The Webs of Time

The Webs of Time

Also by Bruce Macfarlane

Science Fiction

Out of Time

A Drift Out of Time

A House Out of Time

The Space Between Time

The Time Palace of Mars

History

Notes on Arthurian Literature

The Webs of Time

Short Stories

from

The Time Travel Diaries of

James Urquhart and Elizabeth Bicester

by

Bruce Macfarlane

Aldwick Publishing

The Webs of Time

Aldwick Publishing
www.aldwickpublishing.com
All rights reserved

Copyright © 2018 Bruce Macfarlane
ISBN-978-1-9164024-5-4

Preface

Here are short stories from the time travel diaries of James Urquhart, a science lecturer, who lived in 2015 and Elizabeth Bicester, Victorian Cambridge graduate, whom he met at cricket match in 1873.

They are narrated by Professor Rolleston who discovered the original diaries and who spent his life, when not hunting fairies, trying to understand their contents and the reasons for their existence.

$$-- \sim --$$

Three of the stories: Northern Nights, A Holiday in Cornwall, and the Haunted Mill, previously appeared in Three Tales Out of Time.

Moon Shadows first appeared in
A Feast of Christmas Stories: Unwrap a Sussex Tale.

The Webs of Time

Dedication

For
Julia, Heather and Alan

The Webs of Time

Contents

The Webs of Time

On Mars the Waves Are Really High

Introduction by Professor Rolleston.

The creature known by the name 'Peters' appears rarely in the diaries. However I have gleamed sufficient information to conclude that he may originate from an ancient race of time travellers that had the ability to alter time. I am not certain whether his race still exists here or resides in another universe but what is certain is that on at least two occasions he appears in the diaries at a time of imminent catastrophe and is able to move Urquhart and Bicester across space-time without effort to avert the crisis.

Why he and the Martians have such interest in the diarists is an enigma. But no doubt they have discovered that Urquhart and Bicester have acquired special abilities which is advantageous to them.

I hope eventually, as new fragments of the diaries appear, to find how they acquired these abilities for I believe it is key to our survival.

In this narration from the diaries we find Peters has sent the diarists back to a distant past to avert the destruction of Earth and Mars.

On Mars the Waves Are Really High

E.

I'm still not quite sure how we ended up in a time sphere high above the Martian sea watching a ship with its billowing iridescent crystal sails glide across the waves.

But I do remember it started with an outing to Chichester to replace my garments, at James' expense, shredded during our last adventure. The cost had been a little more than anticipated and I felt I should at least treat James to a luncheon in recompense.

As we emerged from the Fountain public house James, whom I had successfully persuaded to leave some beer for the other customers, said. "Isn't Peters' Magic Shop next to the pub?"

The memories of Peters came flooding back to me. He had been our valet on the RMS Campania during our return journey from America where we had helped Mr Tesla revive his health after the disastrous fire which had consumed his laboratory.

The voyage which should have been a quiet, luxurious, romantic pleasure instead, thanks to Peters, left us buffeted about in time again. We eventually arrived safely home at our cottage in Chichester only to find that Peters had left a calling card inviting us to visit his 'Genuine Magic Shop' on South Street. As the novelty of time travel had worn off somewhat we had ignored his offer preferring instead to take a sudden interest in gardening, sewing and watching melodramas on what James called the 'goggle box'.

Thus James' suggestion to look for the shop on this occasion was not met with complete enthusiasm and I replied I did not.

But James, possibly due to his beverage consumption, was not to be dissuaded and said. "I'm sure it was next to the Fountain. Come on. Let's have a quick look."

I followed him, rather hesitantly, to the shop next door only to find to my relief that it was a patisserie. However, despite a rather full luncheon, the cakes displayed in the window looked rather inviting and for reasons which escape me even now I suggested we should purchase some for tea. James, who could consume a tier of cakes without effort, agreed and we entered the shop.

I soon realised my mistake for as we approached the counter, Peters appeared from an alcove!

"Ah! Good afternoon, Mr and Mrs Urquhart," he smiled, "I am glad you could come."

Without replying, we both immediately turned towards the door for escape only to find it locked!

$$--\sim--$$

J.

Considering that I had just demolished a steak and kidney pie followed by jam roly-poly pudding and three pints of the landlord's best I was surprised that I felt the need for cake. But the meringues, chocolates and marzipan displayed in the shop's window were rather inviting.

However on seeing Peters I knew how Hansel had felt on entering the Gingerbread House.

I noticed he'd abandoned his valet outfit and was now wearing one of those dark green worsted suits which you can only buy in one of those shops which sells clothes for pheasant shooters. However, its cut seemed quite old fashioned even by the standards of the game hunting fraternity. There was something not quite right about it. It took a moment before I realised what it was. He was wearing a winged collar! That worried me. It suggested that we may not be where or when we thought we were. This was confirmed when Elizabeth suddenly grabbed my arm and pointing at the shop window said, "Please tell me why, after eating that roast lamb and spotted dick, did I suggest that we needed to buy cake?"

I looked out of the window. The street was filled with Victorians, horses and carriages.

E.

Seeing the street before us I protested that he had entrapped us and taken us out of time. But Peters, if that was his name, replied in a manner that suggested there was no cause for my concern. "Not at all. You may still leave."

James rushed to the door and found it now opened easily. I followed quickly only to discover it led onto the same street we had seen through the window.

"You see," he said, with that helpful smile he had worn on the ship, "You can leave if you wish."

"And how should we do that?" I said quite angrily. "Look at my clothes! I would be arrested in minutes!"

I was wearing a skirt and blouse of the period of James' world which although considered covered up in a modest fashion there, would not be viewed in the same way on the road outside.

"That does present a difficulty which I had not envisaged," said Peters, regarding my form a little too closely. "However if you would come with me maybe we can solve this problem."

He then walked over to a cupboard and on opening it presented us with a small collection of Victorian clothes from the 1890s.

But James was not to be persuaded and said, "Look, Peters, we aren't doing this. Just let us go home to our time."

He thought for a moment then said. "I am afraid I can't."

"What do you mean, you can't?"

"Time has shifted."

"And how did that happen?"

"It was caused by your entry into the shop."

"How?"

"You may have noticed this is a Magic Shop."

"No, we did not!" I said, "It was a patisserie!"

"And it still is. But you came looking for the Magic Shop and now you've found it."

We looked at each other then at Peters.

"So how can we get back?" persisted James.

"It will require a journey on a ship."

"What, another ship? Where is it and where's it going?"

"I have only information on your first question but if you would please follow me, I can start you on your journey."

"And then we can return to our time?" I said.

"I believe so."

"You only believe so? How strong's your belief?" said James.

"There is a high probability."

And he beckoned us to a green frosted glass door at the back of the shop.

"The way to your world is through here." He said, opening the door a little.

I said, "Thank you." And we both walked through.

Why? I do not know. You would think that one of us would have the nous to warn the other of an error in judgement. But I have often found in our adventures that we are of one mind in our ability to 'jump in' so the speak where others might fear to tread.

And thus we found ourselves in a spherical stained-glass room complete with a large green sofa, a heavy Victorian gate-legged table and an array of wheels and dials of the like one might find in the cab of a steam engine.

Unsurprisingly, Peters was nowhere to be found and nor was the door by which we entered.

For a moment we both regarded each other with that look that married couples use to try and blame the other for one's own failings. Then James shrugged his shoulders and said, "Well, let's see what a fine mess we've got ourselves into this time."

And he went over to examine the instruments.

$$--\sim--$$

J.

I was just deciding which lever or wheel to move first when Elizabeth said, "James."

"Yes." I said, still studying the equipment,

"I know you normally only refer to the manual for a device as a last resort," she said, "but in this case I would advise you make an exception, for the instructions are surprisingly simple."

I turned around and saw her studying a piece of paper. I went over and had a look.

It was only one page and contained a schematic diagram of the apparatus. Against various diagrams of wheels and levers were labels marked forward, backward, up, down, future and past. Nothing else.

I took it over to the machinery. It matched.

"It does look simple." I said. "Three levers for travelling about and these two with the clocks for going back and forth in time."

"So we can use it to get back to our world?"

"It seems so. Shall I try it?"

"I wish to say yes. But do you remember how inviting those cakes were?"

I quickly moved my hand away from the time lever.

"So, what are we going to do?" I said. "We can't get out and Peters must have put us in here for a reason."

"Maybe we could just move it a little way into the future and see what happens."

And so without any further thought or reference to past experience, I gently pushed the time lever.

Immediately the spherical walls became transparent, and we found ourselves high in a orange sky looking down at a great expanse of turquoise sea stretching from horizon to horizon.

--～--

E.

I swear I will never enter a patisserie again no matter how inviting its window. Nor, come to think of it, any other shop which displays wares for which I am not in immediate need.

The view of the orange sky and the long lines of impossibly high waves rolling majestically across the sea encompassed the whole sphere and gave me a deep sense of vertigo, if not sea sickness.

James, who seemed to be completely unaffected by the vision, said, "They must have finished terraforming Mars if the northern sea is here. What do you think?"

"I am thinking why did we let ourselves into that shop, pass through a door without question and find ourselves not only out of our time but out of our world. Not to mention...."

I stopped in mid flow, realising what he said, "Did you say Mars?"

"Yep. Look how tiny the sun is. And the sky's orange. We must be in the distant past when the Martian seas first existed."

I steadied myself by the aid of the table as I absorbed the shock of what he had said. It was Mars of course. The sharply curved near horizon and the orange sky. As I watched the majestic waves, impossibly high, roll slowly across the world I became almost mesmerised by their motion. Then a large star about a third the size of our Moon rose from the horizon.

Seeing my direction, James said, "It's Phobos. Look how quickly it travels."

I followed its path. Within a few minutes it was high in the sky.

"Do you know it and Deimos were only discovered in the 1870s?" he said.

"That is strange because I vaguely remember I had read that Mars had two moons before I met you."

"Impossible. They were only discovered by an American called Hall in the late 1870s."

But I was sure I had heard of them before. Then I remembered the story.

"Oh yes!" I said, "It was Jonathan Swift. He described Mars with two moons in Gulliver's Travels."

"Did he? I sometimes wonder whether some of those early fantasy writers were actually time travellers like Wells. What did Swift say?"

"He described an island which floated in the sky by the aid of adamant. And within the island there was a cavern in which a group of astronomers plotted the paths of stars and comets. They described seeing Mars with two moons. They also..."

"Adamant!" he interrupted, "What's that?"

"Why, James! I sometimes wonder how much knowledge had been lost by your time to gain advancement. It was a legendary rock which was often associated with lodestone."

"Oh. A magnetic compass."

"It was more than that. It was said that a piece of adamant, no more than a few feet long, was so powerful that it could interact with the Earth's magnetic field and if you turned it one way it would rise up into the air and if you turned it the other way it would fall to earth."

"A magnetic equivalent of the anti-gravity machine."

"Perhaps. Except a machine as you suggest would have to bend space-time whereas adamant only has to interact with Earth's magnetic field which is far stronger."

To my surprise, he drew me close till our eyes met in that way when we had first seen each other.

"Elizabeth?" he whispered.

"Yes?"

"When, or if, we get back, do you mind taking over some of my lectures?"

"But will I not be burnt at the stake for heresy?"

"Absolutely. Then a few decades later someone will

read what you said and science will take another leap forward."

Although the sciences of James' world are far in advance of mine, the scientists are as bound by convention as they were in my time.

But to return to our fantasy. As we watched Phobos rise into the sky I suddenly I espied a glittering speck of light riding a wave. I watched it grow larger.

"What is that, James?"

He followed my finger. "Must be a trick of the light? Perhaps a wave breaking. No, look! It's getting larger."

"Yes! Perhaps it is a sea creature. But look! It is growing in size. Yet...it does not appear to be moving."

"Strange. Just a minute! It's not getting bigger. I think it's rising from beneath the surface."

After a few moments its shape was revealed. It had the appearance of a galleon but I could not judge its size for there was no reference in the great expanse of sea to compare. Then a mast rose into the air from which a multifaceted sail unfolded. It seemed to catch the wind and billowing in the weak sunshine it glimmered with all the colours of the rainbow. It was beautiful.

We watched it rise and fall on the rolling waves like a child's boat bobbing in the sea.

Then James said, "What are we supposed to do now?"

"I fear that there is only one thing to do. For is it not a coincidence that it appears at the same time as us?"

He nodded reluctantly in agreement and with a resigned sigh he turned to the control panel and gently pushed a lever.

And suddenly we were falling towards the ship.

--~--

J.

I felt like I had just picked up a game controller for the first time. It took a minute or two to get the lever sensitivity right. Pushing the left or right direction levers resulted in us going around in circles and made us quite dizzy as we had no sense of movement. All we saw was the scenery on the walls of the sphere spinning around. Pushing the 'down' lever had us plummeting to the sea which I only just avoided by letting go and pulling the 'up' lever. There didn't seem to be a sensitivity button.

After a few more unsuccessful attempts at flight control Elizabeth decided to help by saying, "I thought James with the hours you play games on your computers in the attic you would have some expertise in this area."

"I do!" I said. "However, the difference is that in my games if I get killed or crash I get another go."

She looked at me as though this was news to her. Then turning towards the spinning scene before us she grabbed the control levers from me. Within a few seconds we were stable and floating gently down towards the ship.

"You see, James, it is hardly different from that

Martian ship we drove into Halley's Comet."

"Yes. I see," I said rather dejectedly as we glided slowly down to the ship, wondering what skills I had left to impress this girl with.

$$--\sim--$$

E.

As we came closer to the vessel, I could see it was over two hundred feet long. From its hull rose strange Romanesque sand coloured turrets pierced by windows which twinkled with the colours of stained glass in the sunlight. The sail seemed to be made of a myriad crystal.

We took the sphere as close as we could but saw no one.

I thought perhaps they could not see us or perhaps we were not really there. However, controlling the sphere to move with the ship as it rose and fell on the waves was exceedingly difficult and I was beginning to feel a little fatigued with the effort and concentration.

I said, "Do you think we should try and land on it?"

"I wouldn't chance it.' said James, "One false move and we'd crash. Let's wait and see where it goes. Pull back."

I manoeuvred the sphere up into the sky again. After about half an hour of tedious though stressful watching, the ship turned a little to the right and increased its speed.

"Either the wind's got up or it's got its own propulsion," said James.

A thin, dark, rugged line appeared on the horizon. As we came closer, I could see dark cliffs and on top of one a red light began to flash. As if to answer the ship turned a few degrees and headed towards it.

"That must be its port."

"Shall we go over to it?" I said. "It might be an advantage to know where it is going."

"Good idea. Do you want me to drive?"

"Thank you but no."

$$--\sim--$$

J.

The flashing light came from a small beacon high up on a cliff face besides a small inlet. We somehow managed to navigate into the gap without damaging anything. It was sheltered from the Martian waves which inexplicably came to a stop at its edge. Around the inlet were small grass-like fields. We found a flat piece and despite a considerable amount of advice to each other on how to control the sphere we landed safely. The vessel arrived about a minute later. It towered over us.

Elizabeth turned to me and said, "So what happens next? I wonder if it has seen us."

Suddenly a bronze tube emerged from the hull and growing in length snaked towards us until the end of the tube seem to connect to the screen in front of us.

It was about ten foot in diameter. And through the screen we could see inside that there was a walkway.

"I think that answers your question."

25

"Yes, but the next question is: are we going to them or are they coming to us?"

"Or," I said, "How about we run away?"

"And where shall we go?"

"What I meant was," I said, "Shall we run away before a horde of little green men come running down that tube with blunt Martian axes and murder us."

"Let us wait a minute. I am sure if such creatures appear, I can lift us up into the sky in seconds."

This is what it's like being with a Victorian girl. No fear. But then, I reminded myself, as Victorian men are prepared to dress up in red and stand in long lines catching cannon balls, their women are going to be of similar ilk.

I said, still trying to find a good excuse to leave honourably, "And supposing that tube attached to the sphere prevents us from escaping?"

"Then it makes no difference whether we go or stay."

See what I mean?

We waited. Minutes went by. Nothing happened.

Then Elizabeth whispered. "As the screaming horde has not appeared, perhaps whoever is on the vessel has placed the corridor for our use."

"And what if it's Martian air inside? It's CO_2 and it's only about one percent of our pressure. We'll be asphyxiated and boiled alive in seconds!"

"Then what else can we do? For as I said before, the vessel appeared when we did. It must be for a reason… we do not know why we are here nor do we have any clue to finding our way home. And…"

26

"OK. OK!" I said. "You've convinced me. Let's go. I suppose we just walk through the screen into that tube."

And that's exactly what we did.

--~--

E.

We left the comfort of one incomprehensible world for another. It was only when James suggested that we were lucky the air was breathable and the right pressure that I reflected on my haste and nearly fainted. Luckily, he did not notice.

The corridor was either illuminated or translucent. I could not tell. It twisted and turned as we cautiously made our way along it so that we could not see more than ten feet ahead. There must have been some strange force at work for I did not perceive climbing or descending. Instead at any point we had the distinct sensation that we were walking on level ground.

Eventually we arrived at what I would describe as an open bulkhead door. James peered in. Then he took my hand.

"Come on."

I am never quite sure whether James is blessed with bravery or foolhardiness. On questioning, he always says he is not brave and says he just tries to take the safest option. I confess this is not always apparent until after the event.

--~--

J.

We were in a small white corridor at the other end of which was a plain wooden door. In its centre was a brass hexagonal knob. I turned it gently and the door swung open presenting me with what I can only describe as the most opulent Victorian hall I'd ever seen. Everything, and I mean everything was covered in ornate, art nouveau woodwork and illuminated by beams of coloured light shining through the stained-glass windows. In the centre a large, wide marble staircase rose up to an open floor of salons.

However, as we stood taking in its beauty, I began to feel there was something familiar about it. It took me a moment before I realised what it was, but Elizabeth beat me to it."

"James! It is the Campania!"

I looked around the hall again. She was right! It was the RMS Campania!

There was one difference though. The hall was empty and silent. Not a soul was to be seen.

Except for Peters.

He was dressed in the liveried garb of the Cunard Line and standing at a table by the stairs holding two glasses.

Once again seeing nothing else to do we walked or should I say waded over to him because we seemed to sink up to our ankles in the Axminster carpet.

"Good evening, Mr and Mrs Urquhart. I am glad you could come. Please, have a drink."

"What's in it?" I said, expecting some potion.

"Lafite Rothschild 1895. I believe it is a good year."

As I'd heard of Rothschild, I tried a sip. It tasted like wine. Then I thought, oh well, here goes and drained the glass.

I was just about to say it wasn't a bad wine but a bit heavy when Elizabeth said, "James! You have just swallowed your annual salary in one gulp!"

"Really? I better have another then while I've got the chance."

To which Peters obliged and beckoned us to sit down.

I started with the obvious questions.

"Why didn't you come with us? What are we doing on the Campania again and what do you want?"

"The first is easy," said Peters. I noticed he wasn't drinking. "I travel a different path to you."

"Explain."

"I mean in what you call Space-Time, I travel a different line which at certain points crosses yours. You could not come here without being taken out of time…"

"You mean we had to use that time sphere to get here?"

"Yes. Although you can travel in time, you are both normally constrained within it."

"OK. Don't quite understand. So why we are we on the Campania again?"

"You are not."

I suddenly remembered my feet sinking into the Axminster carpet. I looked down. There was no carpet!

29

Just the stars.

--~--

E.

I did not think of the price of the wine I had just spilled nor how to remove the large red stain on my ruined dress for I was a little preoccupied with wondering why I was not falling, along with my chair, into the black star-studded void below me.

I looked up. We were still on the ship, if that what it was, sitting around the glass table. Though James, like me, was holding the table rather tightly. It took a moment before I realised Peters had vanished.

Then inexplicably the carpet returned!

"What the hell happened there?" said James trying vainly to remove the spreading stain from my dress. Before I could reply Peters reappeared from nowhere with a cloth and after retrieving my dropped glass and asking my permission proceeded by some miracle to remove the stain completely from my clothes!

When some normality returned, he said, "I apologise for that fault. It should not have happened."

"Why?" I said not a little nervous that something was wrong and that for once Peters was not in control.

"This place is one of many constructs where space-time is in stasis. They are temporarily created to allow communication between species of different times and should be stable."

A little of his normal confidence had disappeared but what he said prompted me to ask, "And pray tell me what species are you?"

"We are similar to you and your Martian friends but much older."

"OK." said James, "That's another box of questions to ask later. But for now, answer my third question."

Peters noticing our glasses were empty proceeded to refill them then said, "You are here because…."

The ship vanished. I mean everything vanished. James, Peters and me! I could not even see my own self!

But I could see the blue green Martian waves coming up towards me.

They crashed into me, silently. The orange sky disappeared. The swirling waters washed over me but I felt nothing except a sense of falling; falling deeper and deeper into the sea.

Then just as I thought I would drown the sea vanished revealing an orange desert in which strange jagged and broken rocks protruded from the surface. I fell towards them and as I drew closer, they looked like islands that had been dropped from the sky.

And then. Snap! I was back at the glass table. They were both staring at me.

"Are you well, Mrs Bicester?" said Peters.

"No, I am not! I fell through the floor into the sea! Down into the depths…"

"When?" said James.

"Just now! Did you not see me?"

"No."

Peters said quietly, "What did you see?"

31

"A drowned world beneath the sea! Then the sea vanished leaving a desert of ruins! Crumbling ruins!"

"We may have arrived too late." said Peters.

"Too late for what?" said James.

"To save Mars."

$$--\sim--$$

J.

I couldn't decide whether Elizabeth had dreamt it or it was real. But she insisted she believed what she saw.

Peters didn't need convincing. When asked what the ruins were, he said, "They were built to defend the planet."

"What from? The third moon that crashed on Mars and caused the Marina Valley and the great Tharsis volcanoes?"

"No. What Mrs Urquhart saw are the remains of a series of floating defensive islands. They were built by my species to defend the planet from the asteroid belt. The purpose of the islands was to bend and distort space and time to prevent Mars being destroyed."

"You mean deflect asteroids from hitting us?"

"Yes. But we had not expected the consequences. The space-time distortions affected the Martian gravity. Each time our defences were used it caused great stress on the planet. As I am sure you are aware, Mr Urquhart, unlike Earth there are no plate tectonics on Mars. The result was that when pressure from the heating core increased there was no surface movement. This eventually resulted in a catastrophic bulging and explosions causing the great fissure across the surface."

"Into which the sea went." I said, "But what happened to the defences?"

"I do not know. The islands fell and were destroyed."

$$--\sim--$$

E.

"Your story is interesting," I said, "but is it not more important to discover why I was shown this vision."

"My hope was that you could warn the islands of the catastrophe they were creating."

"I would have hoped that you would have informed me of that before I was transported there." I said quite crossly.

"I do apologise. I intended to but......."

I interrupted him, "If I understand you correctly, you wished to stop the islands deflecting the meteorites to prevent the opening of the fissure but surely Mars would be destroyed?"

"Mars was not destroyed."

"What?" said James.

Peters said, "Our defences had done sufficient to stop the major meteorites."

"So what can we do?"

Then a thought came to me. "They were your species were they not, Peters?"

He hesitated and looked at both of us. The confidence had gone. He put down the full glass from which he had not drunk and said to me, "Imagine if there is no one left of your species except you and your memories. What would you do if you could change time?"

James said softly and with compassion, "Are you alone, Peters?"

"Yes, and I have all of time. I can go out of time and pass backwards or to the future. But I cannot change time. Only you two due to some quirk, which is beyond my understanding can change the future. That is why the Martians are interested in you."

$--\sim--$

J.

There were a number of problems, but one was important.

I said to Peters, "If we could find some way to warn your people, they'd up sticks and leg it leaving Mars to the meteorites. Is that right?"

"Yes."

"How do we do that?"

And in an instant we were standing on an island a mile above the sea. The orange sky was filled with streaks of multi-coloured light.

We had arrived bang in the middle of the defence of Mats.

$--\sim--$

E.

Sometimes I think James and I should talk a little more before making a decision. Although his suggestion to visit the defences had merit, I could not help but think, regarding the fireworks in the sky and the explosions around us, that the timing of our arrival could have been better planned.

We had found ourselves transported to one of the floating islands. It was virtually flat and covered in a soft green moss. However in front of us was a large dark rocky depression containing a white dome from which emanated beams of shimmering pulsating light into the orange sky. I looked up and saw a strange aberration in the sky as though I was looking through a glass lens or a child's kaleidoscope. Within it great forces were at work for the thundering fire balls which came near it veered off back into space!

"So what do we do now?"

"I think that is for the numbskull who brought us here to decide."

James looked around and finding Peters had disappeared again and realising to whom I was referring, tried to avoid my inference by regarding the cavern for inspiration.

After a few moments in which I thought my nearest and dearest had drifted off with the fairies I said, "Apart from the fiery rocks exploding above and around us do you see anything else of interest?"

This barbed comment failed to penetrate for he was too interested in the horizon which was now lit by the infernal colours of hell and from which a loud rumbling sound emanated.

"The Tharsis volcanoes have exploded!" he shouted.

"Does that mean the seas will vanish?"

"Yes! God! Where's Peters when you need him? Let's get down into this cavern and see if we can get inside that dome."

"Do you think we will be safe there?"

"No idea. Come on!"

We slithered down the rock face like a slow-motion film in the weak Martian gravity. Above us we could hear the roar getting louder.

When we reached the bottom the dome was still about fifty yards away.

"Run for the building!"

On Mars running is not easy and instead we leapt and tumbled across the surface until we both hit the wall.

Before I could recover James shouted, "There must be an entrance somewhere."

The ground was now trembling and loose rocks were cascading down the walls of the cavity.

I swear we ran around the building twice before we found it. A circular panel about three feet in diameter but unfortunately half a dozen feet off the ground.

"Jump!" shouted James.

"We will never reach it!" I shouted above the noise.

"We're on Mars, Elizabeth. Jump!"

And before I could think what he meant, James grabbed me and threw me unceremoniously up into the air. I flew past the portal. Then when I came down again, he threw me up again! I grabbed the panel and somehow pulled it open and clambered in.

36

"Catch me when I jump!" he shouted.

I caught his hand. He was surprisingly light and it was with ease I pulled him in. We hastily pushed the panel shut and the terrible noise outside abated.

$$-- \sim --$$

J.

When I opened my eyes, we were both wrapped tightly around each other's body. Elizabeth's face was buried in my neck. Her perfumed sweat washed over me and for a brief moment I dreamt I was in another world.

Elizabeth stirred and pulling my arms away looked up and around us and sighed with relief.

"God, we are alive."

Around us great mechanical machines whirling silently shot beams of pulsating rainbow coloured lights up through the roof of the dome.

In the centre of the room stood a six-foot-long grey stone cylindrical rock, shaped rather like a weaver's shuttle and supported by four stone feet. Hooped around it was another stone.

However, before I could even begin to make sense of it I thought I heard Peters' voice behind us, followed by a muffled scream from Elizabeth. When I turned, I saw a large white creature, almost like a kangaroo but with reptilian skin. Its tiny hands were like claws. However it was the fact that it wore Peters' face that held my attention.

"What has happened?" it said, I presumed directly in

my brain for its mouth didn't move.

"Your machines have caused so much gravitational distortion that you've fractured the planet surface." I said, "In a short while we'll all be finished."

Its white skin immediately rippled and flowed with the colours of a rainbow like a squid.

"Then we must leave." I heard it say.

Its hands whirred like a fan and the creature suddenly shot up into the air and vanished leaving us alone save for the whirring machinery, meteors and exploding volcanoes.

But worse was to come. I felt strangely light. Elizabeth felt it too. Then I realised what was happening.

"We're falling! This whole damn island is going to crash!"

And as if to verify this, sea water began to cascade down the cavern walls. We were sinking into the sea!

I looked around the chamber desperately trying to think of something then Elizabeth yanked my arm.

"James! This stone! I think it is made of Adamant!"

"Why do you think that? I thought it was a mythical substance." I said.

"In Gulliver's visit to Luputa....."

"You mean Lilliput."

"No! I mean what I say. It was on Luputa. There were floating islands made of Adamant. Remember?"

I gave her my best blank 'haven't a clue' expression. She rolled her eyes.

"Listen! When we first arrived, I said Swift had

recorded the moons of Mars."

"Yes."

"He must have actually seen them!"

"Why?"

"I believe this is one of those floating islands! It is exactly how he described it."

"What?"

"They were supposed to be made of Adamant. Its magnetism counteracted that of Mars. They steered the islands by a rotating stone of Adamant operated by astronomers within a cavity on the island."

"And?"

"That's what this stone is! Look!"

I tried to remember Swift's story but all I could remember were the little Lilliputians and some giants from some place whose name I'd forgotten, mainly because I couldn't pronounce it.

"So why are we suddenly falling?" I said, "If.. oh my God! I know why! There was a theory that a large asteroid collided with Mars and the resultant destruction disrupted the northern Martian magnetic field and its strength dropped dramatically."

"But we have not been hit by such an asteroid. The island defences are sweeping them away."

"Yes! But the defences have distorted the structure of Mars."

"You mean we are falling because Mars' magnetic field is weakening? Then there will be no counterforce to keep the islands in the air?"

"Yes!"

39

"Then we must maximise what is left of the magnetism to break our fall." she said.

"How are we going to do that?"

"Rotate the stone and instead of falling, by opposing what is left of Mars' magnetic field, we may break our fall!"

"Really?"

More sea water was pouring into the cavity.

"Turn it ninety degrees!"

She pushed me towards the cylinder. I grabbed it.

"How? Like this?"

"Yes! Quick!"

It rotated remarkably easily. Too easily, for it slipped out of my grasp and went into a slow spin. My stomach felt weird. Like I was on a swing. But we weren't moving. I grabbed it again and turned it around. My stomach churned. Then imperceptibly at first, I felt myself getting heavier. For a moment outside the sea still surrounded us then it started to drain away until the cavity was empty. I looked up and saw the Martian sky.

It took me a moment before I realised the shooting stars had disappeared.

---~--

E.

I am not quite sure how we summoned sufficient nerve or energy to leave the dome and clamber back up to the surface of the island. Nor how we managed it without slipping and falling back into the cavity. Suffice to say the Martian gravity, fear and an absence of reason assisted greatly.

When we reached the surface, we found the island had settled on a green dank landscape in which pools of sea water were rapidly evaporating. In the deep orange sky, two small moons, one slowly taking over the other rose from the horizon.

Somehow, we had saved ourselves just in time for around us lay the broken ruins of the other floating islands.

And then I saw the ship with its crystal sail billowing in the wind. It came towards us floating magically a few feet above the ground and stopped by the edge of our island.

We ran towards it as you can only run on Mars for a familiar haven is often more attractive than an unfamiliar one.

---~---

J.

Peters was dressed in his Cunard livery which contrasted unfavourably with our ragged and torn clothing. Elizabeth looked like she'd just returned from a party I would have liked to have gone to.

However Peters didn't notice. Instead he cunningly deflected us from our predicament and questions by pouring two glasses of wine and placing them on a large white clothed table

The wine disappeared quickly in silence.

Elizabeth spoke first. "Thank you for that, Peters. but when are we, for I notice the fireballs have vanished?"

He looked pensive and after a few moments during which we thought he had frozen in time, said, "You are now back where you started."

"What do you mean? We've just watched the sea vanish and we're standing in a soggy dessert."

"Look out of the window."

We walked over to a stained glass and through it saw a mountainous wave coming towards us. We and the ship rose with it and over and down again and towards another yet I felt no sensation.

"See? You are back. Now tell me how you saved the island?" said Peters.

"Where do we start?" I said. Then an idea came to me. "Have you heard of or met Jonathan Swift?" I said.

"No."

"Then have you heard of Lemuel Gulliver?" said Elizabeth following my drift.

I'd always thought Gulliver was his first and only name. However, I did not expect Peters' reply.

"Ah! Yes! He came here with a Captain Robinson on the ship, Hopewell."

I said, "So he really wasn't a figment of Swift's mind?"

"Who is this Swift, Mr Urquhart? Captain Gulliver was a capable ship's surgeon and a cousin of the famous explorer Dampier."

"Who?"

"William Dampier, James." whispered Elizabeth, "He was a pirate who circumnavigated the world three times. Surely you must have heard of him? He is famous."

"Well, not to me." I said, "And anyway how did this Gulliver get here from Earth, Peters? I don't remember there were many spaceships in the eighteenth century."

"No. He came here on a small galleon."

"Of course! How else would you get to Mars then?"

Peters ignored my sarcasm but the jab in the ribs indicated Elizabeth hadn't.

"They had been sailing towards Australia," said Peters, "and had stopped at Tonqueen for repairs. They…."

"Where?" I said, still trying to get my head round Gulliver being real.

"I believe in your time it is called Vietnam, James." whispered Elizabeth.

"And I'm beginning to believe I know nothing about anything."

"When they set sail again," continued Peters, "they were blown off course by a storm and accidentally entered a portal which transported them to the Martian sea. They were quite surprised. They had never seen floating islands before."

"Really? Nor Mars I suppose." I said, interjecting a bit more sarcasm which resulted in another jab in the ribs by my nearest and dearest. "Why was he sailing to Australia?"

"He was looking for a fabled material called adamant, a lodestone as hard as diamond. He claimed with this substance he could make things fly."

"Well, he came to the right place."

Peters looked at me in surprise.

"You've heard of it as well?" he said.

"Elizabeth has. Mainly because the swot had not only read the whole of Gulliver's Travels but remembered it as well."

"Long evenings without the distraction of television and internet can greatly aid one's memory, James."

Peters now looked confused.

Elizabeth decided to help. "Your islands are made of adamant. They are controlled by it."

"Ah! I see. I had not realised what you meant."

"But where does the material for the islands come from?" I said. "The only lodestones I've come across are very weak magnets and certainly couldn't hold up an island."

"It is similar to lodestone but it is magnetised by lightning which imparts enormous magnetic strength. It exists in the asteroid belts of Jupiter and Saturn."

"So did Gulliver and his mate manage to get any?"

"When they discovered our islands were made of this substance and how we used the magnetic fields to float above the seas they begged us for some. For they thought that they could use it to make flying ships."

"Did you give them any?"

"Only a little for they quickly realised they could not control it. Too much and their ship would lift out of the sea or start to sink."

"That could explain some of the journeys he took recorded in Swift's book," said Elizabeth.

"Yes. But I wonder where Gulliver's piece of adamant is now?" I said. "Earth's magnetic field is far stronger than Mars. It would have to be tied down well."

Elizabeth suggested: "It is a magnet, you only have to turn it a certain way to reverse its polarity and it would press against the ground."

"Of course," I said wondering why I didn't think of that.

"So, Peters. How have we helped? Apart from warning your species."

"If you had not warned them their machines would have destroyed Mars. As it is, it is in a salvageable state."

"Actually, it wasn't us that saved Mars. It saved itself."

"What do you mean?"

"When the volcanoes erupted, it destroyed the northern magnetic dynamo. With virtually no magnetic field the islands could no longer be supported and they fell to the ground. It was going to happen anyway whether we were there or not."

"But you did save my species."

We stood silent for a moment. I wondered where his people were and how he would find them. I was just going to ask when Elizabeth reminded me of more important things.

"Can we go home now, Peters? I am a little fatigued and hungry."

"Of course."

Once again he seemed to freeze in time then suddenly the hall around us filled with people.

---~---

E.

The journey home was a delight for as a reward we found ourselves completing our journey from New York to Southampton on the RMS Campania.

Though our initial and sudden appearance in the dining hall was much commented on, Peters soon provided us with a new wardrobe and thankfully, when we returned from our state room to dine, no one associated us with the two ragamuffins who had entered earlier.

At Southampton we took the mail coach and our new clothes to Chichester. Unfortunately, a pleasant and cosy journey was, I am afraid to say, mired a little by the Dean of Chichester who accompanied us and spent much of the time bemoaning his work and the popular music played in his cathedral which he thought did not reflect the expected piety.

I must confess after about an hour I felt an overwhelming need to ask him for piety's sake to desist from his sermon but was saved by James who enquired whether I would like a drink.

Before I could answer, he produced a corkscrew and a bottle of Rothschild from his coat. To this day I have been unable to prise from him how he obtained it nor how he secreted it about his person; nor the two crystal goblets which he magically produced from another pocket.

Suffice to say after taking a glass, its soporific effect was such a welcome diversion that I missed the remaining chapters of the Dean's sermon and, as a consequence, potential excommunication from the church.

And that was how Jonathan Swift saved Mars.

There is only one remaining problem. We are stuck in 1895.

---~---

The End

The Magic Shop, the Time Machine and the Martian

The Magic Shop, the Time Machine and the Martian

We were returning home to 2016, a little worse for wear, after a sumptuous birthday dinner for Elizabeth's father when the time machine inexplicably stopped mid-morning in 1895 and vanished.

Luckily, thanks to an excellent and timely six by a batsman, our sudden appearance in the middle of a cricket match in Priory Park was regarded with only passing interest by the crowd.

After about half an hour of wandering aimlessly around the grounds looking for the machine and disturbing not a few people dozing in deckchairs, we gave up and decided to go into Chichester, in hope of getting a clue as to what had happened.

Halfway down North Street I noticed Elizabeth was looking distinctly unhappy.

"Are you OK? I'm sure it will turn up. It always does."

"James, I am dressed for a dinner in 1874 and I've just arrived twenty-one years into the future and find myself out of fashion."

"I don't think your clothes look out of place."

"They would not be out of place if I was twenty years older. But I have already been commented on twice by the young set of Chichester, sporting their ridiculous mutton chops, and wondering why I am wearing the fashion of my mother."

"Is that all? My Victorian underwear is no better. It chafes in all the wrong places"

"Do you want to try a corset?"

"Point taken. God! This place stinks of horse manure and coal smoke. There's no wind."

"I must agree. Your world is so much cleaner. And I miss lycra. Anyway, we must find out why the time machine stopped here. Let us buy a broadsheet and find out exactly when we are."

I went over to a newspaper boy who was shouting the praises of some local dignitary who wanted to build a tramline to Selsea and picked up the local Observer.

"It's the 1st of May, Elizabeth, and ... just a minute look at this. It says people leaving the Fountain on South Street last night noticed a new shop had appeared next door."

"And suddenly on Walpurgis Eve ...how interesting! Any reports of ghouls and flying witches as well?"

"No." I said, scanning the page. "Though the Fountain is supposed to have a ghost of a Roman soldier."

"Did not Mr Wells' family run the Fountain public house at one time?"

"Yes, they did. Aargh, don't tell me he's interfering with our lives again!"

"I would be very disappointed if he is. My evening dress and I have had enough unwarranted attention for one day. But we are stranded in time, and I see no other solution that has sense.

"OK. Let's go and check it out. If he's there he might be able to tell us what's happened."

We passed the Market Cross on our way to South Street and saw a group of people gazing at a shop window. Freshly painted in gold above the canopy, were the words 'The Magic Shop'.

"It looks like we've found him, Elizabeth."

"Yes. But you know, whenever this cursed shop appears, Mr Wells is not far behind with a quest."

I stretched myself over the bobbing heads to see what was grabbing their attention.

"It looks like a model of the Laughing Policeman you get in fairgrounds." I said. "Except it seems to be wearing an orange space suit."

Just then the automaton's eyes swivelled towards us and its hand rose, beckoning us into the shop.

The crowd turned, and following the direction of its hand, stared at us in expectation. I hoped they didn't notice what I was wearing. In my haste I'd left my trainers on.

"Is this your shop, Mister?" said a young boy who looked like he could find and fleece my wallet without effort. I involuntarily felt for it and his eyes followed.

"You want to keep that safe otherwise someone will 'ave it." And he grabbed Elizabeth's purse from a small boy who stood with a cheeky grin holding it up.

I took it, thanked him, gave him a shilling for 'finding' it and told him the shop wasn't ours.

"It looks like the dummy wants you to go in." he replied, "Except we've tried the door and it's locked."

I thought it best not to suggest that if he couldn't open it, I doubt anyone else could.

I took Elizabeth's hand and, wading through the crowd, tried the handle. To our surprise the door opened, followed by an audible gasp from the spectating crowd. We entered quickly and heard the door click shut immediately behind us.

The Magic Shop is always an Aladdin's cave of things you

didn't know you needed. A cross between an ironmongery and the Happy Hippy Shop in Glastonbury.

Wells was standing behind the counter bedecked in his country tweed which, I remembered, he usually reserved only for one of his adventures.

"Ah, Mr and Mrs Urquhart. I am glad you could come."

"I don't remember having any option." I said. "The time machine just stopped here and refused to take us home. Then it disappeared! Luckily we hadn't changed our clothes."

"Yes, Mr Wells. Very fortuitous," said Elizabeth, "I dread to think of my reputation if I had arrived in the attire of the early 21st Century."

"I apologise, Mrs Urquhart, but we are in haste. The Reverend Hilyer has shot a Martian."

"Who?"

"The Reverend Hilyer. He runs a parish church near Trotton. It seems that, on his usual nightly return from the Blue Anchor he saw a witch flying on a broomstick. Being the night before May he thought the devils were abroad and shot it."

"Good God! Is it alright?"

"Unfortunately, I cannot tell you. Hilyer claims it came down to earth and scurried off. He then ran back to the hostelry to get help where, as you might expect, he was met with much hilarity."

"So somewhere there's a wounded Martian. What's that got to do with us?" I said.

"I want you to go back in time and stop him."

"The Martian? What, shall we shoot it before Mr Hilyer does?"

"No! I want you to stop Hilyer shooting it! Mr Urquhart,

I fear you do not always take what I say with sufficient gravity."

"It's my way of dealing with things when I'm way out of my depth. Stress relief. Heard of it? No? It's the 21st century substitute for the stiff upper lip."

Elizabeth interjected with that calm, measured, sweet voice she uses when she is thinking for both of us and everyone should listen. "Just for clarification, Mr Wells, you wish us to return to the night when the Reverend Hilyer is wandering about, in possibly an inebriated state, brandishing a pistol?"

"A shotgun."

"I see. And he is already on the edge of reason fearing ghouls and goblins are abroad?"

"He is known for his interest in local folklore and the fear of the Devil."

"And you require us to apprehend him, disarm him and save the Martian creature?"

"Yes."

"No, thank you, Mr Wells. We would prefer to …"

"Do you remember Woking?" interrupted Wells.

"The Martian invasion?" I said.

"Yes. Unfortunately, if the Martians find out what has happened, they may invade earlier than expected when we are less prepared."

"So why don't you do it?"

"It requires someone who can travel through time without constraint. I do not have that ability."

"But you've seen the future. I've read your books. Wars in the air, tanks, nuclear weapons, to name but a few."

"Just conjecture, Mr Urquhart."

"And this damn Magic Shop appears all over the place

with you in it. How do you explain that?"

"That is not under my control."

"Then what about your book, 'The Time Machine'? You let slip you know Newcomb, the prominent thinker on the properties of time and you have your so-called fictional time traveller argue with him, insisting that time is a dimension, ten years before Einstein will publish his famous paper."

Wells sighed and shuffled some papers on the desk.

"Normally, I only see the future in a dream-like state. When I am asleep, I sometimes feel myself rise from my body and see visions. Terrible visions of the future. But I can do nothing about it, except record my experiences and try to make sense of them. No one would believe what I see, so I write them in the guise of fiction."

Elizabeth said, "This is leading us nowhere, Mr Wells. Even if we agreed to your proposal, how could we help? We have lost the time machine."

Wells rose from the counter and said, "Perhaps I can help you there. Please follow me through this door."

And stupidly, due to either politeness or curiosity, or both, we followed him.

If you have ever been in a forest at night and forgotten your torch, you quickly realise how useful the moon is, if it is up and about. For we found ourselves not in a store cupboard, or even a back yard but on a wide woodland track in the dark.

Apart from a gentle breeze in the tree tops the only other sound was the Reverend Hilyer singing 'Rock of Ages' at the top of his voice as he staggered drunkenly down the road towards us in the moonlight from his evening at the Blue Anchor and pointing his shotgun at anything that moved or didn't.

I looked back the way we had come and found the door by which we had arrived - and Wells - had disappeared.

"Oh, James! How could we be such fools again!" She held my arm tightly. Her perfumed fragrance mixing with the damp air warmed me. "Mr Wells bests us at every turn. We must quit this time travel."

"But you would miss your father." I replied and gave her a protective hug. "And I would miss his port and conversation."

"I know I could not abandon him. But we must learn to think more clearly the next time we meet Mr Wells."

"Well, we are here now. OK. Plan A." I whispered. "Let's hide in the bushes either side of path. You shout out to him and I'll rush him."

"And if I am shot?" she hissed, "Will one of your flying ambulances come swooping down from the future and take me to one of your miraculous hospitals or will I be subjected to an old quack picking pellets from my posterior with rusty pincers?"

"With the padding in that bustle, an elephant gun wouldn't get through. Ouch! Sorry. OK. Let's think of something else."

Just then I heard a loud crack, followed by what sounded like hail falling from the trees above us. It took a second before I realised what it was.

"He's seen us! Run for the bushes!" We dived into the brambles followed by another crack and hail of pellets. We waited while he crashed about looking for us.

"Come out! I know you're in there, Horace!" Hilyer shouted, "Are you with that Rosie again? If the sextant finds out there'll be …"

A bright light in the sky stopped him in his tracks. Which was a pity because I'd liked to have heard a bit more about the amorous Rosie, Horace and the sextant. Looking up, we saw a small iridescent creature with gossamer wings slowly descend and land in front of him. I say land. It hovered in that way Martians do: not quite in this world and not quite out. Hilyer's response to meeting his first alien from outer space was to start singing again, level his shotgun, and fire. All we heard were two clicks. Next moment Hilyer had turned, dropped his gun, and was stumbling hell for leather back to Trotton and screaming that the Devil was after him.

As his voice faded in the distance the Martian turned to us. We slowly stood up. I hoped it didn't know who we were or that we could travel through time. Or more importantly that we knew they were going to invade Earth at some point in the future.

But just as it started to glide towards us, we heard something crashing through the undergrowth. The Martian turned and flew up into the sky. The noise came nearer, and a voice said, "I'd like to borrow your coat, sir."

And before I could reply someone, or something, had grabbed me and pulled my coat off. As I staggered back, I noticed Elizabeth was staring behind me with a look of horror. I turned and saw in the moonlight my jacket. It appeared to have taken on a life of its own and was inexplicably holding and pointing Hilyer's shotgun at me.

"Christ! Is that you, Griffin?" I shouted.

A surprised croaking voice came from above my coat. "How do you know my name?"

"There's only one invisible man I know of. And since the village of Iping is just down the road, I guessed it was you."

56

"I am undone! Give me your clothes or I'll shoot you."

I stood in dumb silence for a second and he pulled both triggers. Click, click.

God! I nearly fainted with fright waiting for the pain. When I recovered, I turned to Elizabeth, but she was nowhere to be seen! Behind me I heard a sickening thud followed by a strangled groan. I thought, he's hit her! I remembered Griffin was supposed to be deranged due to his condition. But when I turned back, my jacket lay crumpled on the ground and Elizabeth was standing over it holding an iron pipe.

"Are you alright, James? You look rather shaken."

"No, I'm fine. I'm always like this after someone has tried to kill me with a double-barrelled shotgun."

"I think I hit him on the head… I hope I haven't killed him."

I felt a little more sympathy for my physical state, rather than Griffin's, would have been appreciated. But then that's what you get when you marry a Victorian woman.

I said, "Don't worry. If you haven't killed him, from what I remember, someone else will. Where did you find that bludgeon?"

"He dropped the pipe when he wrestled with you. I picked it up and was going to help and then he found the gun. When I heard it click, I realised it was empty and rushed him and…"

She dropped the pipe and clasped her arms round me. She was shaking. "God, James! I was so scared. Are you sure you are alright?"

"Yes. Now, where's that Martian?"

"I do not know."

"OK. Let's get back to the road and see what we can

find."

As we came out of the undergrowth, we noticed a shimmering rectangle of light next to an oak tree on the other side of the road. We couldn't run fast enough towards it.

We arrived in a now empty Magic Shop and no Wells. I carefully opened the front door, not knowing what to expect. The crowd had vanished. But as we ventured on to the street, we saw Wells standing outside the Fountain reading a newspaper. As we approached him, he looked up. "Ah, you have returned at last."

"Yes. And thank you for not enquiring after our health, Mr Wells." said Elizabeth.

"There was no need. I can see you are both well."

By the expression on Elizabeth's face I was glad she wasn't still holding that iron bar. But then this was Wells' character. Facts, facts and nothing but the facts.

"So, do you know what happened to the Martian, Wells?" I said, bringing us back to the subject.

"Oh, yes, it had already come into the shop last night to take up its position in the shop window."

"What? You mean the laughing policeman in the space suit?

"Yes."

"So, when you asked us to help the Martian it was already safely ensconced in your shop?"

"That is correct."

"Mr Wells!" said Elizabeth, "We were nearly shot, manhandled by an invisible creature whom I had to bludgeon with an old pipe. James' jacket, which I had only just persuaded him to buy to replace his old one is ripped to shreds. And… you have the audacity to imply all this could be avoided!"

"Let me explain," said Wells, impervious to Elizabeth's outburst. "The Martian saw the Reverend Hilyer was going to shoot it but also saw you had distracted him. When you disappeared through the time door and vanished it surmised you were time travellers."

"How?" I said.

"Martians live in a five-dimensional world. They can see a little of the past and future along the time dimension. It saw where you went and concluded that it only survived because you had come back in time. But for you to come back it realised you had to have a reason for being there. And of course, it knew, what better way to entrap a human than to create the Magic Shop. It summoned me to attend this morning."

"So, how did it find us? We weren't even here!"

"Your machine generates large eddies and distortions in space-time. It wasn't difficult for it to find you and stop the time machine here."

"And if we weren't there, then Hilyer would've shot it and the Martian would not be here."

"Precisely. The invasion might have started. And when you returned to the 21st Century, your world may have already been destroyed by the Martians."

"OK." I said, "We've saved the world for you. Can we go home now?"

"Of course. The machine will be in Priory Park waiting for you just behind the Norman Keep."

As we walked back up North Street, I said, "And to think we only managed to stop Hilyer because we had gone back to 1874 for your father's birthday dinner, Elizabeth."

She looked at me, bit her lip and said, "Did you think Mr Wells told my father to invite us to dinner last night?"

"No. Wells said he can't travel through time."

"Mmm… It is just that my father's real birthday is not until next Saturday."

"What?"

---~---

The End

Entangled in Time

Introduction by Professor Rolleston.
Weber Institute, Mars.

As you are aware from my previous reports, I was drawn to the conclusion that the diarists could not only travel in time but may have existed simultaneously in many alternative worlds.

Here is an example of one where their time lines have somehow crossed with strange consequences.

As usual in my narration, I have joined the diaries together so that the story progresses chronologically from each diarist's perspective and I have assigned a J. for James Urquhart and E. for Elizabeth Bicester for identification.

--~--

Entangled in Time

E.

James and I have been married for over a year now and despite over a hundred years separating our origins I find his world of the twenty-first century a delight. My intimate knowledge of Victoriana has found me in some demand at his college where he delivers lectures on Natural Philosophy or Science as he calls it in his time.

This morning I had risen early, for I had been asked by the Art Faculty to provide a small fashion display of late Victorian clothing at North Park in Chichester. I have, as might be expected, a considerable wardrobe of clothing from that period and it was with little difficulty I was able to choose materials for display though I resisted James' suggestion that a presentation of Victorian undergarments would aid the popularity of my show amongst the students.

By noon I was nearly ready and students were gathering around the marquee on the grass. I was pleased to see that many had entered into the spirit of the occasion and wore an assortment of hired Victorian dress.

I was hoping James would come along to watch. Just after one o'clock, my friend Susan, who runs the Art School and who quizzes me constantly on how I know so much about my era, drew my attention to his entering the Park.

"Is he still wearing that old green coat of his?" she said.

"Yes!" I said. "I thought I had consigned it to charity."

"I told you, Elizabeth, you should have put it on the bonfire."

He looked a little confused. I called out, "Are you well, James?"

He turned in my direction. I waved and after a brief hesitation he came over.

"What is the matter?" I said.

"I'm sorry, did you call me?"

"Yes."

He stared at me as if I were a stranger to him.

"Do I know you?" he said.

"James! Stop playing."

"Playing what? Have we met before?"

"Do you not recognise your wife?" I teased trying to comprehend his game.

He looked to Susan for affirmation. "which one of you is my wife?"

"I am!" I said, "Now that is enough! Come and sit down and tell me how you managed to sneak that old coat into the house again."

He looked me up and down and quipped: "I don't know what's going on but if you want to be my wife I'll be happy to play your husband."

I did not understand this and my patience was

running thin for I had still much to do.

"James! I have no time for parlour games. Come and give us a hand with the seating."

"How do you know my name? Do you know my sister Jill? Not everything she says about me is true, you know."

"What? She is my best friend!"

"Gosh! She's kept you well hidden. So what's your name and what's this wife stuff? I'm not being set up for something, am I?"

I was now both angry and confused. Then a terrible thought occurred to me. Perhaps he was ill!

"James." I reached for his hand and held it tightly. He looked down at my hand then looked into my face. "I am Elizabeth Urquhart. Your wife."

"Hi, Elizabeth. Nice to meet you." He said, struggling to extricate his hand from mine. "Why do you think you're my wife? And why are you dressed in Victorian gear?"

"We are arranging a Victorian fashion show. You remember? I've been working on it for months."

"What do you mean? I don't understand. You look serious."

I was now very concerned for I thought perhaps the sun had induced a brain fever.

I said, "We met at a cricket match in 1873. Remember?"

"OK, that's enough." He said, snatching his hand from my grasp. "I don't know what you're playing at but I've got a lecture to go to. See you sometime."

And then he turned and without even an adieu strode away.

$-\sim-$

J.

I'd finished work late and dashed over to the Art Faculty to see if Elizabeth needed any help.

I found her at the marquee surrounded by a few students who had dressed up for the occasion.

She was wearing the powder blue dress she had worn when I'd first met her. Which was a surprise as I'd thought it had been ripped to shreds during our escape from that Martian round barrow. She must have got it repaired, I thought.

I sneaked up behind her and put my hand around her waist.

"Hi, Elizabeth. I love that dress."

Her scream just about deafened me but was still not as bad as the hard slap across my face which just about bowled me over.

"How dare you, Sir!" Her face was wild. Then she backed off, turned around to the students who were no doubt wondering what old Jimbo had done to upset his wife, and shouted, "Is there no one here who will defend a lady's honour?"

No one moved. Though everyone was looking at me as though I'd just turned up at a wake in a clown's outfit.

"What was that for, Elizabeth?" I said, still rubbing my face.

"What was that for? You put your hands on me!"

"Sorry, your waist in that dress looked inviting."

"How dare you!"

I was speechless.

Then she started. "And how do you know my name? I am sure we have not been introduced!"

"Nor," she continued before I could speak. "Would a mere introduction allow such familiarity."

What was going on I didn't know.

"To answer your question I'm your husband, I hope. James Urquhart."

She turned to the students around us and shouted. "Who will rescue me from this nightmare?"

Then one of the students came over to me.

"How dare you molest a lady, Sir. You cad! If you do not leave I will be forced to give you a blow which you will regret."

And he put his fists up at me like someone who'd just learnt the Queensbury Rules.

"OK. Nice one mate," I said, "but can I have my wife back?"

Then he hit me right on the nose!

I staggered back, clutching my face. There was blood! I looked at Elizabeth who instead of showing any sympathy said, "There, Sir. Perhaps that will teach you a lesson. Now I suggest you leave and go back to where you belong."

"What the hell are you playing at, Elizabeth?"

Two other students approached me in the same threatening manner as the one who'd hit me.

I decided to make a run for it.

I ran all the way back to North Street. A woman looked at me strangely. There was blood running down my shirt.

"Are you alright, dear?"

"Yeah, thanks, I walked into a lamp post."

$$--\sim--$$

E.

After the show I returned home. I must confess I was not pleased with James' charade and I am afraid to say I was determined to give him quite a piece of my mind for his performance. But when I entered the living room, to my horror, he was lying on the sofa holding a handkerchief to his nose and with his shirt covered in blood!

My concern for his condition overrode my anger and I rushed to his side.

"James! What happened to you?"

To my surprise, he pushed me away.

"What do you mean? You were there and egged him on! He punched me right in the nose! What did I do to deserve that?"

"Deserve what? I was upset with your little game but I did not 'egg anyone on' as you say, to strike you."

"Yes, you did!"

"No! I did not! You pretended you did not know me and when I appealed to you....well...you just walked away. I have never been so embarrassed! And in front of my students!"

"What do you mean? It was you who wouldn't accept I was your husband! Jeeze! I only put my hand around your waist and you smacked me around the head. And then you got your students to attack me!"

This was a nightmare. He was lying there covered in blood and accusing me of hitting him and denying I was his wife.

Then he said. "And how come you were wearing that powder blue dress? I thought you'd thrown it away."

"I have!" I exclaimed. "And as you can see I am not wearing it. It was beyond repair after that escape from the round barrow."

It was at that moment both of us realised that something was wrong.

James grabbed my arm and said, "What was I wearing when you saw me?"

"That old green jacket when you first met me and.....oh God!"

"Yes, the one you threw away. And when I saw you, you were wearing that blue powder dress which you..."

".. shredded for rags. So then.. it wasn't me!"

We both stopped open-mouthed. James said, "Precisely - it wasn't us."

"But it was us. Was it not, James?"

"Yes. It seems somehow our alter egos are running around loose somewhere in our world."

I sat down beside him and said quietly, "I am your wife, am I not?"

He looked at me and pulled me closer. "Yes, you are.

God, my nose hurts."

"I hope it is not broken. Let me bathe it and find you a clean shirt."

--〜--

J.

It took a while for us to calm down before we could discuss what had happened. It seemed Elizabeth had met a version of me that had never met her and I had somehow walked into the 1870s and groped her before we had first met. In the circumstances, I think I got off quite lightly.

However, what was more important was there had been some kind of time glitch around North Park which had brought a version of me from an alternative time line and sent me back to Elizabeth's time.

I said, "It looks like time lines crossed. My doppelganger steps into our world and to prevent some paradox I was whisked to your time."

"But it could not be my time, for I would surely have remembered it if it had happened before I met you I met you at the Cricket club." she said.

"You're right. That means both of them are from a different time line."

"But are they from the same time line?"

"Don't know. We could go back to North Park together and see what happens. The time anomaly might still be there."

"Or we could quietly forget all about it." she said.

"And find ourselves in the same state again? I'm in

no rush to be beaten up again by your other self's friends."

"I will be with you to ensure that you don't grope any ladies."

"Thanks. But for some reason I've completely gone off that idea."

"I'm glad to hear it. But anyway, do you think we will find them? Can we all occupy the same space and time?" she said

"I don't know. The problem is what do we do if we meet them? Your bloke isn't going to like you and mine is going to have another fit if she sees me."

"In that case we need a go-between."

"What? Who?"

"Jill."

"My sister? How can she help?"

"One, your alter ego should know her and two, mine will not and therefore Jill will have a better chance of approaching her."

"Sounds risky. But it might work. You phone her. You can explain it better."

"I agree. Give me your telephone."

It took about fifteen minutes of persuasion but eventually Jill agreed to join us at the Old Priory in North Park after lunch tomorrow on the promise of a slap-up meal at my expense.

"OK," I said, retrieving my phone, "Let's see what happens. And because I've watched too many Sci-Fi films, so that we know who is who, I suggest we both carry something that I don't expect them to have and to have a code word that they won't know."

--~--

E.

It took some persuasion to dissuade James from secreting about his person an item of my unmentionables so that I would know it was him and suggested instead we each carried a handkerchief with a message written on it with indelible ink. I also thought a pair of jeans would distinguish me from any Victorian lady who might appear.

We arrived at North Park by the ruined Priory just after lunch at the Old Cross to wait for Jill.

After about ten minutes, James, who had quaffed more beer than he needed, required a call of nature and had to go to the Public Lavatory by the cafe.

I waited for him nearby, trying to ignore the unwanted regard of the people in the cafe who I felt were all looking in my general direction.

Eventually he reappeared.

"Hello again! Hanging about the loo in the hope of catching another husband, eh?"

"I find one husband is quite sufficient for my needs" I said, matching his humour.

"So what are you doing here then?"

I looked at his face. He wasn't smiling. I also realised his nose was not bruised.

My blood suddenly ran cold. I had to think quickly.

"Taking the air." I said, looking over his shoulder, hoping my James would appear but there was no sign.

"Looking for someone?" he said, turning around in the direction of my gaze. "Another husband perhaps?"

I bit my tongue and just managed to desist from answering him in similar fashion.

"No." I replied.

Seeing no further sport he said, "Well. Can't say it's been nice to meet you. 'Bye and good luck with husband hunting."

And he walked off towards the old Norman keep.

As soon as I thought he was sufficiently far away, I rushed into the Gentlemen's lavatory and collided with James just coming out.

He stopped me. "Hey! The Ladies are around the corner. Surprisingly, unisex toilets haven't arrived in Chichester yet."

I ignored his remark. "Did you see him?"

"Who? You mean the other me? No! Was he here?"

"I was just speaking to him! He was quite rude."

"Almost as rude as you were to him yesterday? Don't answer that. Where is he?"

"Walking towards the Norman mound."

He turned in the direction I was pointing.

"God, you're right! It's me! And in my favourite jacket."

Then a thought came to me. "I need to test you, James. Show me the item I gave you this morning."

"I can do better than that."

And to my horror he produced, in full public view, a pair of my black silk knickers!

"Not enough evidence?" he said, carefully ignoring

the expression on my face.

And before I could say anything, he produced the matching bra as well!

"Look, it even has the hook I broke trying to get it off. Convinced it's me?"

The only thing at that point I was convinced about was that the entire 'café's customers were regarding a man waving my undergarments around!

An old couple walking by saw my dismay and the gentleman came over to me and asked if James was bothering me.

I said politely, and without thinking, that he wasn't and he was just looking after my undergarments for me. The enormity of what I had just said and possibly implied only reached me a few seconds later when I noticed the expression on his wife's face. I will not record the conversation that followed with James after they parted. We were interrupted in our lively discussion when Jill arrived.

"Hi, you two. Where're your happy twins then?"

Noticing what James was carrying she said to me, "I don't want to pry, Elizabeth, but why have you given James your underwear?"

"I have not!"

"Wow, that's an impressive skill you've acquired, Jim. I hope you're not going to teach that trick to Sean."

Jill and I had long ago decided that her boyfriend and James were not to be trusted together and were only allowed out under licence which they invariably tore up as soon as they were out of our sight.

"He brought them with him." I said.

"Why?"

Suffice to say the conversation spiralled quickly downhill along with any remains of my reputation until he, whom I sometimes refer to as the love of my life, eventually explained to Jill why he had them and also that carrying ladies' undergarments like trophies about him and displaying them to all and sundry was not his usual habit.

Unfortunately, due to the distraction of the last few minutes the other James had disappeared, as Jill pointed out.

We ran towards the Norman mound but although we circumnavigated it thoroughly, we found no-one. We were about to give up when James, who had hidden my garments in his clothes again, whispered, "Look up there!"

And there was his twin standing on top of the mound looking straight into the children's playground where, swinging slowly back and forth on a swing boat, was my twin wearing my powder blue dress!

James turned to Jill and said. "OK, this is it, Sis. Go over to her and see what you can find out. We'll be waiting for you over at the café. Honest!"

-- ~ --

J.

I couldn't figure out what was going on. I'd just left her by the café and now there she was on a swing in the playground wearing those Victorian clothes again.

I decided to get a closer look and climbed the mound where I could watch her from behind the trees.

--~--

E.

I had arranged to meet my sister Flory in the park for tea. While waiting for her in the café I noticed nearby several children's swing boats had been recently erected. I had not been on one for years and a devilish impulse to try one came over me. I carefully climbed into one and pulled on the rope to allow myself to swing to and fro in the afternoon sunshine. A young lady appeared. She was about my age but dressed in a fashion suggesting she was a circus acrobat. Noticing me she came over and introduced herself rather informally.

"Hi. I'm Jill. Are you Elizabeth Bicester?"

"Yes, I am. Have we been introduced."

"In a way, yes. Are you waiting for someone?"

I ignored the manner of this personal inquiry and replied, "Yes. I am waiting for my sister. But I must apologise as I cannot recollect your name."

She hesitated before saying, "I'm Jillian Urquhart. You may have met my brother, James, yesterday."

The awful event of yesterday came back and the anger which rose with the memory caused me to reply rather rudely.

"I certainly have! He molested me! No doubt that may be usual amongst you travelling people but not in my society."

Instead of rising to my implied slur on her character she responded rather quietly.

"Do you feel your surroundings are rather strange?"

I looked around. The swing boats were new but other than a distinct absence of coal smoke rising from the nearby domestic chimneys I perceived nothing different. An incredible noise came towards us from above. I looked up and a great machine with a large rotating propeller appeared and flew over us. I covered my ears. It was deafening.

"What on God's Earth is that?"

"A helicopter."

Her words were meaningless. She saw my expression and said, "Oh, sorry. It's a flying machine."

"A flying machine? Where did it come from?"

"From my time." She said with a smile as though the infernal contraption was the most natural thing in the world.

I could not comprehend her answer. "What do you mean, 'from your time'?"

She did not reply but instead opened her handbag and produced, after much rummaging, a thin black plate on which she began to prod repeatedly with her fingers.

"Oh! there must be a picture somewhere. Ah! Here it is."

She showed it to me. It contained a miniature of that Mr Urquhart!

And, incredibly, I appeared to be standing next to him in a short skirt, bare legs, revealing blouse and no hat or gloves! And to my horror, my arm was around his waist!

"What trickery is this? Is this a circus forgery? What are you and your brother after? I am sure I have done you no wrong."

She grabbed my arm.

"Please! I mean you no harm, Elizabeth!"

"I am Miss Bicester to you!!"

Just then I heard a sound above and looking up saw her brother by a tree on top of the mound. He was spying on us!

"Let go of me!" I shouted, trying to pull away from her grip for I feared I had been set up to be robbed or worse.

"Elizabeth!" she said. "I mean Miss Bicester. I am trying to help. You are out of your time! Look around you. The helicopter! Is this your world?"

Then she said to herself. "God! What have Jim and Elizabeth got me into now?"

I looked around me for help and noticed her brother coming towards me. He was holding and waving a white handkerchief in his hand as if in surrender.

$$--\sim--$$

J.

As I watched her swing to and fro, to my amazement my sister appeared, walked straight over and started talking to her. I was too far away to hear what they said. But then Jill took out her phone and showed it to her. I don't know what she saw but the girl recoiled in horror. At which moment I tripped over a root. They must have heard me for they both looked up and saw me. I thought it best to go and join them. The only thing I could think of doing was to get out my hanky and wave it in the air hoping she would understand I meant her no harm.

When she saw me she tried to run away but Jill caught her arm and started arguing with her. I couldn't help but notice how very pretty she was.

-- ~ --

E.

When he approached I noticed that he was smiling apologetically and said in a similar vernacular to his sister. "Hi. I'm sorry about yesterday and earlier but I didn't understand the game you were playing."

"What game? I was not playing a game." I said. "You were!"

His sister interrupted. "Right! Shut up both of you! You obviously haven't a clue what's happening. Now don't say another word because I'm going to tell you what's going on and you are both going to listen and believe it!"

Her brother and I both stopped in our tracks.

"Good! Now first thing is, as far as I'm aware, until now you two have never met before, so any argumentative baggage you brought about each other is irrelevant. Understand? No? Tough! Second, this person," pointing at Mr Urquhart, "is not my brother in this world. My brother's over there with his wife."

I looked over to the cafe where she was pointing and saw, to my amazement, a second Mr Urquhart with a woman who looked remarkably like me except she was dressed like another circus trollop!

"Thirdly." she continued, looking very vexed and pointing rudely at me. "You were groped, as you call it, by my brother because in this world you are his wife. He put his hand around you as an affectionate greeting."

Before I could reply she turned and, pointing at Mr Urquhart, said, "Whereas you, Mr Urquhart, met my brother's wife" pointing at me again. "She was pretty pissed off that you denied her marriage to you. But not as pissed off as my brother was, who when he mistook you, Miss Bicester, for his wife" pointing rudely at me again, "you set your friends on him. Got it?"

It was at this point I turned to Mr Urquhart for help and found to my surprise he was regarding me with the same bemused expression!

--~--

J.

My sister had gone mad.

"What are you up to, Sis?"

"I'm not sure I am your sister, ! I told you. Your sister, Jill, is me but has followed a different time line Think about it! All this stupidity is because you've all jumped into each other's timelines. Got it!"

Sherlock Holmes came to mind but he didn't help because thinking through what she said, I realised that

79

the only possible explanation was the impossible!

I said, "If what you say is true how do we get back to our own worlds?"

"I've no idea. But I strongly recommend that you first help Miss Bicester here to find her world because she won't last five minutes in the 21st century."

Miss Bicester grabbed my arm then realising what she'd done removed her hand immediately.

"This is the 21st century?" she said.

"Yes!" I said, "You saw the helicopter?"

Then the penny dropped. She looked around her. "Then I am lost! Help me get back, Miss Urquhart!"

"I can't. And besides I've got my own two idiots to look after. I can't cope with four of you!"

The girl looked genuinely scared. I couldn't walk away. I said to her. "Are you willing for me to help you?"

She looked at my 'sister' then at me and after some hesitation nodded.

"Good." said my sister's twin, "Now, I'm going to leave you both and get back to my two before they get into more trouble. Or even worse, I drop out of this time. Good luck. You'll have fun."

And she walked off in the direction of the café.

We stood alone together in the children's playground. I looked at her closely for the first time. For a moment I thought I was looking at a Tissot painting of one of his idyllic ladies. Then she broke my reverie.

"I feel you are regarding me with too much attention,

Mr Urquhart."

"Well, you shouldn't look so pretty."

Her eyes widened. "Is that how you entice a lady in your century?"

"No. Normally we just sneak up behind a girl and put our arms around her waist."

For a moment she looked startled and I thought I'd gone too far. But then a smile flickered briefly across her face.

"You are very foolhardy, Mr Urquhart."

"My sister says I'm very foolish." I said trying to return a smile.

"I can see she has reason."

I couldn't tell whether she was being serious or playing with me. I tried moving to safer ground.

"Tell me about yourself, Miss Bicester?" I said.

"Is it not normally polite in your society for a gentleman to introduce himself first to a lady?"

I'm sure I sensed her voice soften and those eyes were giving me trouble.

"Er.. You know I don't know. OK. I'm James Urquhart, a simple science lecturer living in Chichester."

"Thank you. And I am Elizabeth Bicester, daughter of the Squire of Hamgreen."

"A bit posh then?"

"I have no idea what you mean by that, Sir."

"OK. Fair point. And what are you doing here?"

"I might ask the same of you."

"I was on my way home."

"And that required climbing to the top of that mound, hiding behind a tree and spying on me?"

"No! I thought I'd just talked to you by the café wearing jeans and then suddenly you were on the swing thing in that blue dress. I didn't understand!"

"So you thought you would observe me secretly."

I'm sure I detected a smile.

"No! I mean yes." I said, "I thought you were the other one!"

"That is hardly an excuse."

"No, it's not. Sorry."

We stood there silently until she said, "But in the circumstances you describe, I think curiosity would be."

"Would be what?"

"An excuse. For it would be a singularly uninteresting person who could resist exploring the phenomenon you observed, would it not, Mr Urquhart?"

She looked me straight in the eye as though she was waiting for an answer. I didn't know what to make of that. I couldn't figure out whether she was goading me or giving me a compliment.

Then she said, "To answer your question. I was waiting for someone."

"Well, it looks like they've got a long wait. What year are you from?"

"Pardon? Oh. I understand. I was... living in 1873."

"My God! Really? So that's not just fancy dress."

"It certainly is not! I presume you too are wearing appropriate apparel for your era, Sir?"

"I guess I am."

"I am surprised you are not wearing a hat?"

I pulled out my cap. "Here it is."

"Then should you not be wearing it? Is it not bad manners to appear in public hatless?"

I involuntarily did as I was told. "That's better." she said. "Now are you going to take me home or must I find it myself?"

I had a distinct feeling I was being judged on how singularly uninteresting I was.

"I'll try. But I don't know how. You may end up stuck in this world with me."

"Would that be a problem for you?"

She was definitely goading me. I was just about to tell her so when she came closer.

"Mr Urquhart," A faint but delicious perfume wafted over me. "It seems in one world you are in love with me and in another I am in love with you. Does that not tell you something?"

What game was this? I replied rather defensively, "Is that how you chat up men in your century?"

"In my world a lady would not 'chat up' a gentleman, as you say."

A picture of Burne-Jones' painting of Merlin being beguiled by Nimue came to mind.

I said, "I bet she'd leave a trail for him to follow though."

Another smile.

"I could not possibly comment." She said, giving me a look, which suggested she just had!

I noticed she hadn't moved away. We stood silently looking at each other. A breeze blew through the trees on the mound, rustling the leaves and the scent of her perfume seemed to become stronger.

I said, "OK. I'm up for it. Now which way do you think we should go?"

"We could ask my sister over there."

"What? There's two of you? Where?"

I turned towards the direction she was looking. But instead of finding our twins by the café I saw an open carriage with two dappled grey horses and beside it stood another girl in a yellow Victorian dress waving to us.

"Are you coming?" Elizabeth asked. "As your other sister said, we might have fun."

"Are all Victorian ladies this forward?"

"Who said I was a Victorian?"

"But I… I thought you were from….."

"This is no time for thought, Mr Urquhart. Now come on before time changes and we are lost in another world where we have to start all over again."

Then she put her arm through mine and guided me towards the carriage.

For some reason I didn't mind.

--~--

The End

Time Fracture

Introduction by Professor Rolleston.
Weber Institute, Mars.

A difficulty with assembling the diaries into a chronological order is that many are fragmentary and originate from different time lines. It is akin to constructing a jig saw puzzle of a picture with pieces from a number of puzzles all of the same image but cut differently.

But there are some which do not fit at all. Their stories end strangely as though the time travellers were somehow trapped or caught in a temporal eddy.

Perhaps you can better understand what I mean by reading the following example:

--~--

Time Fracture

J.

We were enjoying a quiet evening together.

Elizabeth was snuggled up in my favourite chair by the fire reading a book my sister Jill had left her and I was half dozing on the sofa. I had dimmed the lights a little to enjoy the dancing shadows cast upon the walls and ceiling by the flickering flames from the hearth.

As I lay there contemplating nothing in particular, apart from her delectable green-embroidered-stockinged calves, she suddenly looked up and glanced around the room with a rather puzzled expression. But before I could ask what was the matter she whispered:

"James, do you think there is something wrong with this room?"

I looked around and noticing perhaps that a few improvements could be made said, "Do you think it needs redecorating or some new furniture?"

"No. It is not that. It is very comfortable. I wish for nothing more."

I was about to joke that was the reason why I married her when I saw in the shadowy light something was worrying her.

"What is it?"

"There is something different."

"Is it the fire?"

"No, it is very cosy. But... but I feel somehow the

room has been turned around … as though everything is topsy turvy"

I looked again; this time with a little more concentration. Everything seemed to be in its place. I glanced at the clock on the wall and then my watch. They both said 9:15.

Elizabeth noticed my actions and quickly looked at the clock as well.

"Are they as they should be, James?"

"Yes. They seem to be."

"Then perhaps it is nothing," she said, relaxing a little, "Do you think a nice cup of tea or cocoa is in order?"

I took my cue and rose from my comfy sofa and wandered over to the door to put the kettle on.

I don't know whether you have looked at the stars in a clear frosty sky on a winter's evening. They twinkle magically.

However, I did not expect to see them when I opened the door into the hallway.

I felt the hair on the nape of my neck tingle. A black star- studded firmament stretched out before me. I blinked. It was still there. I decided to carefully close the door as if nothing had happened and try it again. But too late - I heard a sharp intake of breath from Elizabeth behind me.

Her voice was almost a hiss. "James!"

"Yes?" I replied in almost the same way. I turned slowly. Her eyes were wide, staring, but to my surprise, she was not looking at me or the door, but towards the window.

"We have a visitor." she whispered almost inaudibly.

I moved my head slowly following her gaze. Then I saw it. It was looking at her.

The creature was ghostly white, only about three feet tall, very thin and floating above the ground. It was disconcertingly familiar like a character from Lewis Carroll. The head was like that of a cat but its ears were more like a rabbit's. Its eyes were wide set and bulged and blinked like a frog's. Protruding from its shoulders were two small wings which seemed to shimmer iridescently as though they were not part of its body.

It began to drift slowly towards Elizabeth. She was motionless as if mesmerised. My mind screamed telling me to protect her but I couldn't move! It was now very close. She sat there frozen white like a statue. Even the colour in her clothes seemed to be draining away. Then it extended a hand and as it gently touched her body, to my horror they both vanished!

--~--

E.

My recurring nightmare that one day I will wake and James will not be there beside me has happened! I know I am from a different time and I always fear that the strange bond that holds us together will weaken or break, transporting me back to my nineteenth century world for ever. But I did not expect this!

I now found myself alone with a creature from another world floating above a valley bathed by the light of an orange star-filled sky in which hung two small silvery moons. I immediately realised where I was though I could not comprehend how, for on the horizon, impossibly close, rose the three great Tharsis volcanoes of Mars.

I turned to the creature still in shock from my abduction and said, my voice quivering, "What do you want of me?"

In response I felt its hand hold mine. I instantly tried to withdraw but was unable. Resigned, I waited for the ghostly reverie which normally accompanied their touch. but instead I heard it say, "Elizabeth."

It knew my name!

"Have I said it correctly?"

"Yes,"

"You and your..your…."

I interrupted it angrily. "My husband? Remember? How dare you take me from him! Where is he?"

But it ignored my remarks and continued as if I had said nothing of consequence. "Both of you, like us, can travel out of time. But unlike us you can travel in Time. Therefore, you must find your way back to Earth and unjoin Time."

"What do you mean unjoin?" I said.

"You know how."

Before I could ask 'how' I was supposed to know, its wings shimmered with the colours of a rainbow and the creature vanished.

Now I was really alone and to my consternation it was getting dark. The shadows cast by the weak sun on the valley walls were lengthening and the great volcanoes were now a deep orange. I felt panic rising. I could not at first think what to do but then remembered the Martian cavern we had visited in the time device was nearby. But where? The light in the valley was fading fast. I tried to recall how we found it but as I thought it, as if by magic, I was there!

It was the same cavern, but it was empty. No ship or time machine. I looked around in hope but found none and in my despair and rage, I shouted, "And what is it I am supposed to do now?"

$$-- \sim --$$

J.

She's gone! The blasted creature had taken her. What do they want this time? I looked at her empty chair in disbelief and then at the door. I realised there was only one way to find out. I walked slowly over to the door and very carefully opened it. The dark sky was still there but to my relief the air didn't rush out of the room. Nevertheless, I took a deep breath before I walked into the unknown.

As I stepped through the door I found myself in a silver-grey landscape illuminated by a full moon shining high in the sky. About a hundred yards in front of me was what looked like a grass covered mound. Seeing nothing else of interest and noticing rather disconcertingly that the door through which I had come had disappeared, I decided to walk towards it. The air was still and warm like a summer's evening. But as I approached the mound I realised it looked familiar. By the shape of the stones guarding the entrance it looked like the West Kennet long barrow. If it was then I knew where I was though not how I had arrived there. I climbed over a small grassy ridge and approached the two largest stones where I remembered there was an entrance. At first I couldn't see a thing for it was in the shadow of the moon. But then as my eyes grew accustomed to the dark I saw a pale green light. I peered between the two stones and saw an illuminated passage. Seeing nothing else to do I squeezed between the stones and entered.

The passage was narrow, low and lined with large rough-cut stones. I stooped down to avoid the roof and walked slowly along it guided by the soft glow until I came to a small chamber from which three even smaller chambers radiated. It was lit by the same green light. I could not see its source but it seemed to come from the walls themselves. I carefully looked around the chamber but it was empty. Until that point I thought I was on the path I was supposed to take but I suddenly thought that maybe my journey was somewhere else in this world. I felt a cold sweat on my back. In a panic I methodically prodded and probed the stones in the hope of finding a hidden portal or something; but found nothing. Then just as I was about to give up, a ghostly white light filled the room. As I looked up I banged my head on a stone. When I'd wiped away the tears I saw the moon shining through a gap in the roof.

I turned around cautiously and noticed that the light had caused a pattern to appear in relief on one of the wall stones. There seemed to be three cuneiform markings. I touched one. Then the others. Nothing happened. I pushed and prodded them with no effect until I realised that perhaps I had watched too many SF and horror films of secret passages opened by hidden buttons and locks.

Nevertheless, on examining them more closely I had the distinct impression they reminded me of something. But as I stood there contemplating their meaning and rubbing my bruised head I heard Elizabeth's voice which caused me to look up sharply and smack my head again on the same protruding rock!

--~--

E.

I nearly jumped out of my skin when I heard James reply, not least because of the language he used.

"Jeeze! I've banged my damn head again! Where are you?"

"On Mars."

"God! What the hell are you doing there?"

I am not sure in a normal couple's relationship, if one exists, the husband on hearing his wife has been abducted and transported to another planet would reply in such a manner.

I said with some concern, momentarily forgetting my predicament, "Are you not well, James?"

"No, my head hurts and I'm not happy."

"Where are you?"

"I think in Wiltshire in a burial mound."

My heart sank. I had hoped he was close by.

"So what do we do?" I said.

"No idea. How did you get to Mars?"

"The Martian brought me here and then said I have to find my way back home!"

"Is this their idea of a game? Where is it?"

"It vanished!"

"As in 'dematerialised'?"

"Yes."

"Didn't give a plan?"

"No!"

A brief silence ensued during which I hoped my beloved was hatching a plan for I could think of none.

However, his reply did not bring comfort.

"OK. Situation here is: I'm in a chamber with three symbols on a large stone. I've tried pressing them all but they do nothing."

"What do they look like?"

"Well, one looks like a circle with a cross. Another is an arrow and the other a circle with a dot in the middle."

"Oh. Are they not the signs for the Earth, Mars and the Sun?"

"What?" he exclaimed.

"You know. The astrological signs of the planets."

There was another short silence, followed by James replying, rather testily I thought, "Remind me what my job is again, Elizabeth?"

"I understand the college sometimes give you a little remuneration for talking about the stars and planets."

"And do you think that might include knowing what the symbols of the planets are?"

"I would not know, James." I said, and hoping to bring a little humour into our predicament, "It is not something that would normally fill the head of a dutiful Victorian wife."

Another long moment passed and then he said, "Would you mind if this conversation was not repeated?"

"Of course."

I will, of course, keep it as a little treasure for after dinner with our friends if we ever return home. Poor James.

"So having established I'm an idiot, what do you think I should do now?"

"Perhaps you should align them so they are in the positions they are in the sky now?"

"And how do I that since I can't move them?"

There was a note of annoyance in his voice, no doubt caused by his injuries. I felt it best in order to progress to play a more feminine role. I replied, "I am at a loss, James and feeling very alone."

This had the intended effect. "Oh. I'm sorry for shouting. Are you OK? This is a bit stressful. Anything your end?"

I looked around the cavern. It was bare save for a single door. A door! I am sure I had not noticed it on arrival. I shouted "James! I have found a door!" and ran towards it lest it disappeared. Unfortunately, I had forgotten the effects of the lighter gravity of Mars. It is generally accepted, though I expect James would disagree, that ladies in skirts should not perform cartwheels in public and I was glad there was no one there to observe my rather immodest predicament after bouncing off the wall and landing sprawled on the ground. I was also relieved there was no one there to hear the language I used for which I blame prolonged exposure to James.

--~--

J.

As I stood there looking at the rather 'obvious' symbols and wondering what to do I noticed the chamber was getting darker. I looked up, carefully avoiding the protruding rock and noticed that the moon was passing across the hole in the roof. I realised it would disappear soon.

I turned to the stone and in desperation pressed the symbols again in the fading light. Nothing. Then the moonlight vanished and the chamber went black, really black. I couldn't see a thing. I leant against the wall with a sense of hopelessness.....and.... fell straight through it!

--~--

E.

Having rearranged my skirts to some form of respectability that would sufficiently allow me not to be passed off as a strumpet after a successful evening, I examined the door.

To my surprise, there were the three symbols that James had found next to the door and like him I pressed and prodded them to no effect.

I called to James. "Can you hear me?"

"Yes. I'm in a tunnel! What have you got?"

"I have a door with similar signs. They do not respond to my touch. What do you think I should do?"

"No idea. Does the chamber look the same?"

I looked around. I saw nothing unusual if you regard such a thing as not unusual.

"No, it looks the same"

"And when you push the door nothing happens?"

"Oh!"

I gently pressed the door and it silently slid open to reveal a small ante-chamber. Whether it had been unlocked all the time, I do not know. For a moment I could see why we married each other. No one else would tolerate such fools.

As I cautiously looked into the tunnel I heard him say, "I gather by your silence that trying the door was not something you'd considered."

I tried to defend myself, "I fear the distraction of my abduction has left me with only half my wit."

"Well, the other half of your wit, if you trust him, would like you to enter the chamber and see where it goes."

-- ～ --

J.

The tunnel was quite short and ended at a blank wall. I walked up to it and cautiously pressed it with my hands. To my relief, I watched them disappear through the wall. I followed them and walked straight through. When I recovered, to my surprise, I found myself in a large chamber. I recognised it immediately. It was the Time Cavern at Midhurst! There in the centre were the large, five-foot-wide, illuminated globes of Mars and Earth, and above them the bronze dials of the time controls. They showed the year 2015.

I walked over to the Martian sphere. The 3D detail on its surface was amazing. I could see the deep green canyons cutting across the orange Martian deserts which discharged their waters into the northern Martian sea. I looked closer and could almost believe that I was looking at the real world for I was sure I could see the waters moving. Then I noticed a small brass pointer floating above the Tharis Volcanoes at the end of the Marina Valley. I touched it and nearly jumped out my skin for a thin blue line emanated from it and rose into the air.

I stood back and watched it slowly grow and traverse to a point on the Earth's globe. I followed the blue line to where it had landed and found it had joined a similar brass pointer on the Earth's surface. It was Midhurst. Were they showing our locations on Earth and Mars? If so then maybe this was showing somehow a way across the worlds!

I shouted, "Elizabeth I'm in the Time Cavern! Just go into your chamber and with a bit of luck you'll see a blank wall. Just walk through it and you should end up here."

--~--

E.

I followed his advice though not without a little hesitation but to my relief I found myself in the Time Cavern. Except, James was nowhere to be seen! I called out. "Where are you?"

"I'm in the Time Cavern."

"So am I but I can't see you."

There was a short silence. I wondered if I had imagined his voice. I looked around the room. I was alone save for the worlds of Mars and Earth floating in the centre and next to them were the controls which on previous occasions we had used to travel across time and space.

Then I heard him again, not in my ears but in my mind.

"What's the date on the time controls?"

I examined the dates on the brass dials above the globes, "It says 1873... oh, do you mean...?"

"Yep. We're in the right place but different times. It's 2015 here. Keep still, I'm going to come to you."

I waited. Again, the silence. The second hand on the time dial slowly rotated. Then his voice. "I'm now in 1873. What's your exact time and date?"

I gave it to him down to the last second. I waited

again.

Then I heard him. "You're still not here. Oh God! Don't tell me we are on different time lines."

Oh, so close! I imagined the loneliness of us drifting through alternative times hearing each other but never to meet. Then a thought distracted me, "Perhaps they cross over."

"What! Oh yes of course. You're a genius. Worth a try. Well, there's only one way to find out. I'm going back to 2015 and then I will slowly go back to your time and you come to mine."

"But the intersection could be any when!"

"Damn! You're right. It could take forever. Oh, this is not fair and my head really hurts and I miss you. Just a minute let's try 1895 when Wells published 'The Time Machine'. He's usually lurking about then when we start travelling about in time."

James had reason. Mr Wells did seem to favour that year. For over an hour we crossed that year back and forth with I confess not a little cursing until suddenly James appeared. Oh, the relief! But as I rushed to embrace him I noticed he was not alone.

--~--

J.

In some way I was not surprised to see H. G. Wells again, nor he to see us.

He was wearing his tweed country clothes complete with plus-fours and a matching flat cap.

"Well done, both of you." he said with a smile.

Judging by Elizabeth's expression she would have had him 'well done' with her hat pin.

"So, Wells, what have we done this time?" I said.

"You have joined time."

"How?" I said, not looking forward to the answer.

"There was a time fracture which caused the link between the portal on Mars and Earth to break. It required the creation of a new time line to allow us to travel between the two planets."

Elizabeth and I looked blankly at each other, but Wells ignored our expressions and continued.

"As you know the Martians can see a little into the past and the many futures that exit, and thus can observe how we travel through time. They saw that at the fracture literally all time lines stopped and concluded they could only be joined by threading a new time line through the fracture. But that required the sowers, so to speak, to be either side of the break."

"And that was us, I suppose. Why couldn't we just do that together?"

"They looked at your future time lines and the only one which met with success was the one where you were separated."

Elizabeth turned to me. "That's why the creature said we would know how. They already knew we would succeed!"

I said to Wells, "Wouldn't it have been polite to ask first rather than just abducting my wife and frightening the wits out of us?"

"Unfortunately, prior knowledge may have generated new time lines that were not foreseen."

I whispered to Elizabeth, "We're going to have start charging for our services." Then turning to Wells. "So are all the old time lines joined together now?"

"Good Lord, no! That would be far too difficult."

"So for everybody the past is different."

"Not too much that you would notice. The shift at the fracture was not great but sufficient to stop time flow."

$$--\sim--$$

E.

Although as usual we did not understand everything, the relief of being together again was more than sufficient compensation.

However, there were two things that perplexed me. I said, "What was the purpose of the symbols we found on the walls, Mr. Wells?"

"What symbols?" he said, looking a little perturbed for a change.

I described them.

"I have no idea. All I understood was that you had to discover the portals and walk through them."

"And also, how could we talk to each other?"

"Simple. In their five-dimensional world to which they had taken you, you were next to each other all the time."

Time? I had experienced enough Time for one day. I said, "So, Mr Wells. Now you have used us to save the world again, may we go home?"

"You already are." And he pointed at a third door which for some reason we had not noticed before.

J.

I found myself in the hallway of our home. There were no stars. Everything was normal. Nevertheless, I quickly opened the front door and was reassured to see my car was parked on the drive.

I returned to the parlour where I found Elizabeth already snuggled up in my favourite chair. I went over to her and kissed her gently on the lips. She looked up in surprise and said smiling "Oh, that was nice and rather unexpected."

She went to return my kiss but noticed my head. "Oh, you have bruised yourself. How did you do that?"

My mind raced. I looked at the clock it said 9:15. No time had passed!

"Are you alright? You look a little startled."

I said as calmly as I could, "Oh, it's nothing. I walked into a wall."

"You poor thing. Let me make you a nice cup of cocoa."

She rose and walked towards the door. The door!

I quickly followed and grasped her hand and said, "Let me come with you."

She turned and squeezed my hand in return and with that beguiling smile of hers said, "Am I on a promise, James?"

She opened the door.
The stars twinkled magically…

--～--

The End

Three Tales Out of Time

Introduction by
Elizabeth Bicester

On a number of occasions when we found ourselves at home from our time travels, James' sister and her boyfriend Sean took us on holiday in his carriage. One would think that such pleasures would be a welcome distraction but you will see that things do not always turn out as expected.

--~--

Comment by James Urquhart.

If you ever find yourself going out with a Victorian lady and you feel the need to impress her with your romantic skills, I would suggest taking her night clubbing in Hartlepool, camping in Cornwall or touring in the remote parts of France should be immediately crossed off your list.

--~--

Northern Nights

J.

Hartlepool is a bleak and windswept place lying on a promontory on the north east coast of England. It's battered by freezing winds from what Elizabeth still calls the German Sea which come down from the Arctic to chill the bones of anyone who wasn't born and raised there. When the sun does come out it is immediately followed by sea fog or frets which percolate far in land and can last for weeks while the rest of the country is on the beach soaking up the sun. Its inhabitants are divided by the "Slake"- a natural harbour. Those on the headland are called "Cods Heads" renowned for their fishing abilities and those in the town are known as the "Monkey Hangers." When they meet the conversation usually begins with a preamble concerning the whereabouts of the other's father at the time they were born and the number of men of the town their mother or wife are "known" to.

The "Monkey Hanger" appellate seems to have originated from the Napoleonic wars when a French ship was wrecked off the coast and all were drowned save a monkey. Apparently the good and patriotic people of Hartlepool had never seen a Frenchman before and mistaking the monkey for one, hanged it. Most people would have kept this deed quiet for fear of embarrassment. But not the people of Hartlepool. Even today a picture of the hanged monkey is proudly displayed on the ties of the local rugby club and the local football club's monkey mascot has recently been elected as mayor of the town!

--~--

E.

We were travelling up to Hartlepool with Jill to meet her boyfriend Sean for the weekend who had been attending an exposition there. For our stay he had managed to acquire temporary accommodation for all of us at favourable rates in the small fishing village of Seaton Carew not three miles from the town where we could enjoy the seaside air whilst regarding the clouds of black fumes rising from the steel works and blast furnaces of Redcar.

I had not seen the great industries of our country before and when I saw the gigantic factories and tall chimneys stretching to the horizon as we passed over the River Tees I realised that much of what I depended on for comfort and enjoyment did not come from the surrounds of my home in Sussex.

When we arrived James and Sean, after much discussion, decided that as it was my first visit to Hartlepool they should show me "a good time" in the town and proposed for the evening's entertainment one of its exclusive clubs that apparently one reads about in celebrity magazines. As my experience of a 'good time' had recently been limited to the fashionable set in Chichester who normally retired by the hour of ten I thanked them and said I looked forward to broadening my horizons. It was agreed that "Club Gemini", better known amongst the posh as Twins, should be the place of choice. I had not come across any reviews of this fashionable place even though I had been trying to keep up with 'modern' society by reading Jill's magazines and listening to "Woman's Hour' on the radio which for some reason lasted from ten o'clock in the morning to four in the afternoon and informed me about a lot of things I didn't know I should be worried about.

So with no more ado and a quick change of dress we were off.

Well actually we did not dress quickly as I am afraid to say there was much discussion between Jill and me on what to wear or to put it more succinctly, what not to wear. It seems to be considered fashionable in Hartlepool for an evening just wearing one's undergarments was regarded as overdressed. I was not to be persuaded though and insisted on wearing enough to leave sufficient for the imagination.

--~--

J.

The streets were quite empty as the usual gaggle of women who had passed out earlier on the pavements due to misjudgement of the quantity of alcohol in a bottle of gin had been carefully removed by the local constabulary.

We arrived eventually at Club Gemini and after receiving a cursory inspection at the door by the concierge, who looked surprisingly like the French monkey and distinctly gave me the impression that I had personally hanged his great-great-grandfather, we were allowed in.

What a sight greeted us. If there is a God and I'm allowed a glimpse of heaven I think his work would be cut out to improve on the view before us.

--~--

E.

I had never been in a bordello but if you asked me to describe one I think the sight before me would have provided an adequate impression. I can only say that as we passed through a heavy curtain I was greeted by a sea of semi-naked gyrating doxies of various sizes wearing clothing that would have brought a blush to a dollymop. They seemed to be dancing to a fast, loud and rather repetitive form of African music emanating from the ceiling. I say seemed to be dancing for I saw no one who understood the correlation between the musical tempo and the movement of their bodies. In my time, in order to be able to dance at a ball or soiree, it was customary to wait until asked by a gentleman. Here no such requirement was needed. In fact, I saw groups of men, shirtless I should add, gavotting by themselves with no regard to the half-naked strumpets around them. I could not begin to imagine, in my time, how much consternation, not to mention disappointment, would be engendered amongst the mothers of young debutantes who having prepared their daughters for a ball for over a year in the hope of attracting or palming them off to the men of their choice found themselves confronted by these dancing monkeys.

James has told me that it is a well-known fact that there is a high correlation between how much clothing with which a woman will cover herself and the availability of men in her town. When I tell you that apparently most of the men in the town either worked at sea or spent their evenings in their working men's clubs you may get an indication of the vision that met our eyes.

I noticed James was quite enjoying the scene though when questioned he insisted that he much preferred me to be dressed the way I was. Sean, however, who had lived in a country for some time where in general women wore more sober attire, looked distinctly unsteady on his feet.

--~--

J.

At some point there was a general announcement by what looked like the door monkey's cousin that there would now be a "Sussies" Competition. This was met by screams of delight and a general rush to the stage by dozens of women of all ages.

A group of the more attractive and less inebriated ones managed to clamber on to the stage and to the whistles and roars of the mainly female audience proceeded to lift up their skirts and dresses to reveal a surprising variety of stocking tops and suspenders.

Well, I realised now what is meant by the seven steps to heaven. Up to now I had obviously only been on the first rung!

--~--

E.

Words fail me! Not least because James and Sean suggested that we should join in this competition. When I questioned them about being asked to join a line of drunken strumpets showing my ALL as though I was on display in a brothel for the whim of its customers James said it would have no effect on my reputation as we would not be coming back the next evening. Realising by my look that he had now overstepped the mark by some distance he then tried to mollify me by saying that if I had worn my red embroidered stockings, (I have come to suspect a vision of me wearing such items and nothing else occupies a significant part of his brain) I would have won the competition hands down. I thanked him for thinking I would do well in this line of work but said I regarded a bottle of cheap champagne as not sufficient incentive to join those trollops on the stage. I was also pleased that Jill declined their suggestion to join me in a rendering of that infamous interlude from Offenbach's operetta. Though when I questioned them on why they thought I should do this to my horror James said he had 'heard' from my cousin Henry that I had performed quite a remarkable rendition of it while at Girton. How that story got out beyond the walls I have no idea but I will interrogate my sister Flory very closely next time I have the opportunity to meet her.

--~--

J.

By now Sean needed to be propped up by Elizabeth and me. She told me later that he didn't blink his eyes for almost 20 minutes and was unable to answer even the simplest questions such as "would you like a drink?" or "May I remove that dead cigarette hanging out of your open mouth?"

Eventually when the display of fine legs and lingerie had finished our girls suggested we leave before our eyelids became permanently attached to our foreheads. They guided us reluctantly back to the exit and out in to the fresh air. When we arrived back home and recounted the evening in detail lest we forgot anything Jill sent Sean upstairs and told him not to come back down until he had thoroughly washed himself in bleach and carbolic soap, for it seems that the reputation and habits of the ladies of Hartlepool were already well-known to him.

--~--

E.

The following morning after this exceedingly late evening Sean decided we should all go off to Whitby, the well-known fishing village on the Yorkshire coast to taste what he called the heart stopping cuisine of a famous fish and chips emporium and to look for vampires. I thought he was still a little light-headed from the previous evening's excesses for my only knowledge of such creatures were in the laudanum filled minds of Byron and his friends but nevertheless he seemed to be quite in earnest so we agreed.

James also thought Sean looked a little peaky and eventually persuaded him that he should hand over control of the car. Though I must admit he did not look much better.

--~--

J.

We were driving along towards Middlesbrough, a town whose only claim to fame was that it had been voted second worst place to live in England, and were admiring the view of the billowing clouds emanating from the cooling towers of Europe's largest chemical works and enjoying the fragrance from the local incinerator and River Tees at low tide, when Sean suddenly announced he was feeling a bit queasy.

With quick dexterity he managed to wind down the window in time to give one of the best projectile vomits I have ever seen. Unfortunately, the back windows were also open. Personally, I was never very good at fluid dynamics at college but I expected better of Sean who had trained to be a meteorologist and should have understood the subtle nature of wind, vortices and laminar flow. Instead of spraying and improving the surrounding countryside of Teesside, the substance travelled in a backward direction. To be fair some did go out of the window but most inexplicably returned through the back window.

I was conscious of a deafening silence from the rear compartment where Jill and Elizabeth were sitting. I pulled over and slowly turned around to see if they were alright. I don't know whether you have seen one of those machines which spray pebbledash onto houses in England but the apparition before me reminded me of the effect that one of these machines could have on human beings. Though where the diced carrots came from I don't know as I did not remember our eating them at dinner the previous evening.

For some reason the girls just stared at us without a word which continued for quite some time while we endeavoured to clean their clothes and the car.

--~--

E.

After we had returned to Sean's apartment in silence, washed ourselves and changed our clothes we were persuaded to return to Whitby for this Jill and I agreed was by far preferable to experiencing another 'good time' in Hartlepool. As it was getting late James said we should book overnight accommodation there and reserved a place by telephone. I am pleased to say that the second journey to Whitby that day was uneventful and the fish and chip supper supplemented by endless quantities of buttered bread and tea went some way to remove the odour of that morning's exploits which for some reason followed us across the moors.

Once refreshed Sean said we should go and look for vampires. He said that apparently a certain Count Dracula who was of this ilk had landed here by ship inside a coffin accompanied by what Sean called his female assistants. Legend had it that he was buried in the grounds of Whitby Abbey and as it was nearly dusk and vampires only come out at night an ideal opportunity to meet him had arrived. I had read a little of these creatures and although I had come to the conclusion they were figments of the deranged minds of Polydori and his friend Byron, the abbey silhouette by the evening sky on the cliff above cast a little doubt in mine.

Legend also told there were hundred and ninety-nine steps up to the abbey from the quay on which it was said no one had counted more than one hundred and ninety-eight. For if you found the last one a local superstition recounted the devil would appear and snatch you away. Sean said he had found there was a hundred and ninety-nine steps every time he had climbed up to the abbey but so as not to invoke 'Old

Nick' he had always stopped counting at one hundred and ninety-eight. How Jill coped with his blarney I do not know.

--~--

J.

When we got to the top we wandered around the graveyard looking for signs of Dracula. We eventually found one that had a large skull and crossbones on it and all agreed that was where he was buried and we could desist from looking around furtively in the shadows for him. We were about to return when I noticed the Methodist chapel behind the wall and Sean suggested before we depart we have a quick look inside.

Inside the chapel it was now quite dark but we entered nonetheless, our footsteps echoing on the wood and tiled floor. At the end of the hall we noticed what looked like coffins on trestle tables. As we approached I counted four and that they were open for the lids were carefully stacked against the wall. At this point normal people stop, make excuses about remembering a previous engagement and leave immediately. Not Sean. "I must have a look." He said. And walked across the floor and looked in the first box. He then turned with an expression I imagine he had when he first saw the apparition of the Pope on the bedroom wall of his grandfather's house in Kerry and then to reinforce what we already feared shouted at the top of his voice, "They're empty!"

Nothing would change our opinion that the Count

and his female servants had risen from those coffins and were now loose amongst us. We left and walked very fast, no, to be truthful, we RAN back to the steps. I am sure there were more than two hundred steps back down but I did not count nor look back.

--~--

E.

I arose early in the morning for some solitude to write up my diary primarily to ensure that at a later date they would confirm that the memories of the last two days were not the result of a short and pestilent fever. It was still quite dark. As I entered the kitchen I espied what I thought was a small figure on the stove. I instantly froze for the previous evening's escapade was still fresh in my mind. I turned slowly and saw not the Pope, as Sean had recounted he had seen at his grandfather's house as a child, but the Virgin herself! I am not of the Catholic persuasion and do not normally suffer the guilt which that particular religion encourages in its flock but at that moment every misdemeanour I had done against the teaching of God flashed into my mind. I was surprised how many came flooding back before I remembered I was also living in sin!

--~--

J.

The scream from the kitchen and the absence of Elizabeth next to me had me out of the bed in an instant.

"What's the matter?" I said as I reached the hallway

and saw her outline in the kitchen.

She was staring and pointing at something behind the kitchen door. Telling myself to keep as calm as possible and trying not to imagine that Dracula or one of his maid servants had found our apartment, I entered.

My exclamation wasn't quite as loud as hers but gave the same impression. There was the Virgin Mary standing on the cooker!

This is not good news for an Atheist for I believe the punishments for breaking God's commandments are nothing compared with denying his existence. And for a moment there in front of me was proof that he did exist, or at least his mum did.

But as I contemplated this, and more importantly how I was going to form an apology for doubting in him, sanity returned. I moved closer. I was reprieved! It was just a painted alabaster figure of the Virgin.

"Sean!" I shouted.

"What's the matter?" He said when he eventually staggered in dressed in what I can only describe as Wee Willy Winkie's nightgown.

"What's this?"

"What? Oh that. I'd bought it in a shop for me mother and left it in the car. I thought I'd bring it in for safe keeping."

--~--

E.

It is not often one hears in the presence of an image of the mother of God such a stream of profanities as James released in the direction of Sean. I must confess

I agreed with many of his sentiments even though I didn't understand all their meanings or exactly the direction of their biological application. Suffice to say I could only hope that the Virgin, whom I noticed on the stove was looking quite shocked, would forgive us when she realised this little episode had prepared her in good stead for her arrival at Sean's family in Kerry.

--~--

The End

The Haunted Mill

E.

In certain seasons northern France is enchanting. The roads, empty of traffic, meander through meadows and fields of maize and sunflowers which seem untouched by hand since the time of Henri the "Bon Roi". Beside the roads, lines of tall poplars shelter you from the burning sun which James informs me were thoughtfully planted by the inhabitants to allow "les Allemandes" to march in the shade.

We had been travelling on such a road for most of the day and by late afternoon the blue sky had begun to fill with billowing white cotton clouds so familiar to those who live in a maritime country and which often herald the arrival of rain and storms. For our voyage we had taken Sean's carriage and within this the four of us idly talked about times past and new adventures. The carriage had suffered many dents and bumps from the excesses of traffic and bollards but did not seem to mind, though even by the standards of modern driving, the poor car seemed to have had more than its fair share of these knocks and scrapes. However, any who have witnessed Sean in Chichester shunting his car back and forth between two vehicles to make space for parking would not have been surprised.

119

We had just emerged from a small wood and arrived at a crossroads when the car suddenly coughed, spluttered and came to a halt.

--~--

J.

I was just nodding off in the warm afternoon sunshine when Sean's car decided to interrupt my solitude. The engine had come to the conclusion that it was unfair that it should be doing all the work and had decided to take a break as well for first one cylinder then another gave up the ghost. The other two, quickly seeing an opportunity for a rest, came out in sympathy. Sean and I looked at each other and then at the car. This had no effect. He tried the engine again but it would not go. After about the fifth attempt we turned to Elizabeth and Jill for encouragement but quickly noticed they were looking at us in that quizzical way which ladies do when they wish their men folk should just not sit there but DO something.

Seeing this had little effect on us Elizabeth thought instruction was needed and said, "Do you not think, James, you should look under the bonnet and try and ascertain what has happened?"

Finding no argument against this suggestion we reluctantly got out and lifted the car bonnet. Why? I do not know but it is customary for a man whose car has broken down to lift the bonnet and to twiddle and prod various components of the engine using "expletives" and engineering words unknown to anyone but himself. After a few minutes we gave up and Sean took the only course of action available and lit up a fag. (By that I mean a cigarette and not a habit possibly well-known in pre-Brexit Referendum days to the English prime minster, his chancellor and the Mayor of London). This was unobserved by the ladies as the bonnet lid hid us from their gaze save for the tell-tale blue smoke that rose into the air which we hoped they would imagine came from the engine.

Finishing his fag and wiping our hands on the greasy engine in a pathetic attempt to convince our companions we had carried out a comprehensive examination of the engine we returned with glum faces.

Unfortunately, by their close questioning they quickly realised that we had come to the end of our mechanical expertise and Jill said, "Well, before you cover yourselves further in grease to no avail I think phoning a garage for help might be in order."

Now a telephone: it's such a simple thing. I have one in my pocket now. However, when you are in one of those many places where mobiles do not work one must use a real one connected to a land line. You remember those don't you?

However, in certain parts of France this is a difficult quest. First you must find one. From the comfort of the car try as we might we couldn't see any. Then Jill thought perhaps we should get out of the car and walk down the road as this might improve our chances of finding such a device.

By 'we' I should add she meant Sean and I.

Ensuring that the ladies were reasonably comfortable

and had sufficient provisions for their needs we set off to find a telephone. After walking for about a mile I became convinced that we were in a '*departement*' where laws had been passed to ban the use of telephone boxes. Another half mile and Sean had decided that the law had also been extended to people for there was no-one to be found. Eventually, after another half mile which included crossing a small ford we arrived at a typical French village. I reminded Sean that Napoleon had accused the English of being a nation of shopkeepers and to ensure French villages kept their unique identity, with the exception of cafes and Tabacs, shops were '*interdict*'. Sean agreed but added that he believed an exception was made for '*boulangeries*' providing they closed before the normal hour of rising in the morning.

We entered such a village and crossed the square to the cafe. Sean opened the conversation as he told me he had done a course once on the French language. After a number of efforts, we were provided with two shots of coffee accompanied by two shots of some liquor which on swallowing took the back of our throats off. When the red mist and tears from my eyes had receded I noticed we hadn't progressed very far so I had a go.

"Do you have a telephone? You know, a telephone?"

To emphasise my requirement, I then put one hand to my ear and the other performed small circular motions in the hope that it gave the impression of dialling. This charade seemed to work for the patron pointed to a black apparatus covered in fag ash and wine stains in a dark corner connected by two wires to the kind of electrical circuit breaker you would normally only find on a nuclear power station. However, for a few euros and some more Franglais, by pulling down the lever on the circuit breaker it was possible through the miracles of French telephonic engineering to be connected to the outside world. Unfortunately, everyone on the receiving end seemed to have taken up the French language. No doubt another edict from Mr Bonaparte. But just when I had given up the *patron* came over and said,

"Can I help you?"

I had not realised until then that I could understand French! I replied as only a person who has visited a number of countries and acquired a little of their languages can do.

"Excuse em moi but donde esta is une garage? Nos car is not marching."

The *patron* looked at me. I could see by his expression he was thinking very deeply and that it was a habit not too familiar to him. To reinforce my opinion, he looked up at the ceiling where I presume in the room above he was hoping God was there to help. Then on receiving what I thought was an appropriate sign turned to Sean and said,

"Would you both mind speaking English so I can understand you?"

There was then a little confusion on our part as we tried to continue in our best Franglais until it became apparent that the use of the language of communication he suggested could help immensely in our quest. For we found once we reverted to our native tongue he ascertained our plight very quickly and then demonstrated the advantage of being bilingual by phoning his brother who knew a bit about *voitures*.

It took us some time to get back to the car mainly because Sean was convinced that when we departed from the cafe we should have turned left rather than right.

--~--

E

After about an hour we began to wonder where James and Sean had got to and I speculated they had found a *Routier* where they had been enticed into a five course meal with copious quantities of local *vin* and completely forgotten about us. Jill thought that it was more likely that they had found and fallen in love with a couple of French hussies and abandoned us. However, just when we had given up hope and were considering throwing ourselves at the first rich Gallic *homme* who would take us away to his French chateau, an old truck arrived and a man in a thick woollen vest alighted and asked if we were friends of the strange foreigners who had told his brother that their car had broken down. When we said yes, for some reason, he offered his sympathies and suggested that if we wished to move to France he would introduce us to some bon *amies* who had a modicum of sanity and would look after us properly.

Before we could answer in the affirmative he went to the front of the car and performed some operations which indicated that opening a car bonnet and examining the contents was his life and joy for he quickly told us that a machine called an '*alternateur*' was broken. I was just going to ask what this was when we espied our nearest and dearest walking or should I say sauntering along the road towards us with an air as if they did not have a care in the world.

--~--

J.

While we were walking back the effects of the shots of alcohol began to take effect. This gave Sean the opportunity to quiz me about Elizabeth. Not knowing about our time travel adventures I had to be careful.

"So, Jimbo, I hear you found Elizabeth at a cricket match. Is she not a bit posh for you? A bit different from your usual slappers, I hear."

"Careful, Sean, you're talking about Jill's friends."

"Good point, we'll let that pass. So what's the attraction? She's a bit stuck up at times."

"Just the way she was brought up. But underneath she's just like the rest of us and she certainly keeps me on my toes."

"Oh. So she really goes, does she?"

I find answering this question about a girl you're in love with quite difficult to answer. First you want to demonstrate to your mates that you're an alpha male and there is no harem big enough to satisfy your desires but at the same time you want to demonstrate that this is the best girl you've ever had (Sorry I meant 'met'. Oh dear, I meant 'had' and 'met'...I'm in trouble if she reads this, aren't I?). There is also the problem of ensuring that she is viewed as a girl of moral upstanding and is not the local motorbike just in case any comments you make get back to her.

Luckily Sean saw my hesitation and was good enough to help me not dig a deeper hole. So he said.

"Well, Jill likes her. She says she's good for you though I don't normally take that as a compliment from a girl. What I don't understand is where do you disappear off to for days at a time?"

"She hasn't travelled much so I've been taking her around the country."

Just then luckily I noticed a truck by our car and what looked like a mechanic talking to the girls.

When we got back to the car the mechanic was conversing fluently in French with Elizabeth. I realised in hindsight that I should have taken her instead of Sean to the village and saved some embarrassment. When she saw us she said,

"Where have you been, James? The *garagiste* could not find you on the road and was worried you were lost."

Sean, who was not going to admit to taking the wrong turn, said we had gone into the bushes for a pee and must have missed the mechanic.

"Well, James, I hope you are feeling better. Anyway, I understand the *alternateur* is broken and it will not be until tomorrow that a replacement can arrive and the car should be taken to his garage for safe keeping."

How she translated or even knew the word 'alternator' I have no idea. However, this news resulted in a little quiet mumbling between Sean and me on the competency of French engineering. Maybe the word "Agincourt" came up. But just when we were discussing the advantages of arrow over armour, Elizabeth, who like all girls can multitask and therefore apparently can listen to two conversations at once said, "James, before you start a new Anglo-French war I should tell you that this "*bon homme*" has offered to take us to his house for some supper where his wife will give us a delicious homemade broth and a welcoming glass of Calvados."

All discussion of Agincourt and Crecy were quickly forgotten. And so, having hitched Sean's car to the truck, we jammed ourselves into the front seat and were whisked off to the village we had just left to the mechanic's house.

After excellent hospitality, where Elizabeth translated and thankfully filtered all the conversations, I asked her to see if they knew where we could stay and to our amazement she said the mechanic had told her we could rest overnight at an old mill nearby owned for many years by their family and that his wife and daughter had already left to prepare for our reception! We graciously accepted his offer and I asked Elizabeth to tell them that we thought the French were the best people in the world and would tell everyone so when we got home.

--~--

E.

We transferred all our luggage to our mechanic's carriage and in no time at all we were off into the countryside to the old mill. However, this contraption was nothing like Sean's and I promise not to complain about Sean's carriage ever again. To begin with a door was missing which allowed us to enjoy the fragrance of the recently chicken-manured fields and the roof seemed to be made of a roll of corrugated iron. The suspension was so over sprung that each corner rose and fell independently of each other and in the process transferred our luggage from one lap to another. It was only by sheer willpower and the fact that the carriage was designed only for four that we remained wedged in our seats. I asked James what this devilish machine was and he replied that it was a Two Cee Vee so named because it had the power of two horses. I suggested that if I had horses that gave such a ride they would be in danger of being turned to glue at the earliest opportunity. He agreed with me but also said it was such a difficult car to maintain that in the past, before we had met I should add, his second question to any prospective girlfriend was whether she owned one. Apparently he was quite convinced that a woman who had bought such a carriage was only looking for a man who could service it for them. He then unnecessarily reminded me that in forming a relationship with a lady, servicing her undercarriage rather than her carriage was normally his preferred objective. Well really! I reminded him that although most women suspected the thoughts of men ploughed a deep and rather narrow furrow I did not need further confirmation. For some reason he found my reply quite humorous!

However, by now it was getting very dark. There were no lights save the weak beams of the bone-shaker illuminating the narrow road. After about half an hour we turned on to a narrow gravel track. Dense hedgerows pressed against us casting strange shadows in the dark. There had not been any signs of habitation for the past few miles. How long we travelled I do not know but just as I began to think that perhaps Sean's comments on French engineering and Agincourt had been overheard, the "*chemin*" cleared and a silhouette of what we took to be the mill surrounded by decrepit old ruined barns and outhouses appeared, momentarily illuminated by a gibbous moon scurrying through a gap in the clouds.

--~--

J.

We stopped at some distance from the mill and the mechanic got out. He beckoned us to follow him and also pointed out to avoid the large dark pond to our left which we hadn't noticed. After an exchange of glances, we retrieved our baggage and followed him carefully as he guided us with a torch towards the mill. The night was silent, not even an owl, save for the sound of our feet crunching on the gravel. We followed him up some rather rickety steps and arrived at a porch. He then pushed open the unlocked door and striking a match lit an oil lamp which revealed an old oak beamed room which looked as if it hadn't changed since the parting of heads of the French nobility from their bodies had become fashionable. He quickly went round the chamber lighting candles and oil lamps then beckoned us in. I didn't even think it was worth asking whether there was any electricity.

He showed us around the chambers and a small kitchen and then leaving some matches on the table with a parting adieu he left us and drove off into the darkness. The old mill was now very quiet and ours.

--~--

E.

There was no sound save for the gentle rustling of invisible trees tops swaying in a light wind. James thought it was very romantic. I reminded James that in my time when one lives on the edge of comfort one does not seek a dilapidated old barn for a holiday.

Sean thought we should light a fire for no other reason I believe than fire lighting had come into his mind. James also thought it was a good idea as well even though Jill reminded them it was the middle of August and I suggested that one had to be careful in lighting fires in old wooden buildings in high summer.

There is something about boys and matches. It is a habit which stays with them all their lives and I can only presume it comes from a past when a man who could light a fire had some advantage over his fellows in attracting a mate. I could see the advantage of this but it has been some time since my criteria for a male companion included his pyrotechnic abilities. Nevertheless, Sean and James obviously still thought this was the way to a girl's heart and insisted on treating Jill and me to a demonstration on fire lighting. With much excitement and tales of previous pyrotechnic adventures our menfolk piled anything that was combustible into the grate. Then gathering an old newspaper Sean crumpled it up, pushed it under the wood and, taking a match, lit it. The paper burnt wondrously but inexplicably the wood was not interested in joining in. James then said he remembered his dad holding a newspaper over the fireplace to get a good draught going. I have seen this done many times at home with usually some success. More paper was gathered, crumpled and lit. However, I presume James did not have an adequate grip because first the centre of his newspaper turned black followed by a circular orange hole. Before I could say anything the paper set alight and flew up the chimney!

But they were not to be defeated. Sean found some liquor and proceeded to pour it on the wood and tossed a lighted match on it. Jill tried to stop him but too late, for with a rather disconcerting whoosh, the wood ignited at such a rate that burning embers flew out on to the hearth and up the chimney.

A mad panic ensued accompanied by much admonishment of a certain two idiots accompanied by a discussion between Jill and me on why we let them into our beds as we stamped out on the embers and smouldering rug.

Eventually we extinguished the fire and decided that no further experiments in this area should be carried out if we wished to avoid burning down the mill.

Then for some reason, still inexplicable to this day Sean decided that we should pass the time recounting our favourite ghost stories.

"I'll go first," said Sean before we could interrupt. He looked around the room as though he was looking for some unwelcome phantom to materialise and moving closer to us he said in almost a whisper,

"You know what worries me about this place is it reminds me of an old haunted house my grandfather had when I was young boy just outside Killarney."

I said. "And why do you think it was haunted?"

"The Pope would visit us at night."

"The Pope!"

Yes. Just as I be getting off to Fairyland I would see glowing by the door a figure. It'd get brighter and brighter until I could see it was a luminous head."

"What did you do?"

"I went screaming off to me grandpa who said don't worry it's only the Pope."

"The next night there he was again! His eyes would follow me. It was horrible. I only stayed there three nights and refused to go back again."

"Gosh, Sean, that must have been scary. Did you find out what it was?"

"Yes. Apparently the Pope and his entourage had turned up in Killarney for Mass which was well received. Except they'd turned up at the local

Protestant church by mistake. There was hell to pay and it said he cursed the whole county. And from then on figures of the Pope started turning up everywhere."

"What a terrible curse, Sean. I'm not convinced I would want to experience such an apparition."

To which James replied,

"Elizabeth! Don't believe a word of it. Its typical Sean blarney. It was just a luminous picture of the Pope on the wall. His grandad used to rent the place out to tourists. There was one in each room powered by a small battery. It was hidden just by the door. When the occupant closed the door there it was."

"Is that right, Sean?" Said Jill. "You had me believing you!"

"They're everywhere in Kerry." continued James, "You can buy them from the Nuns shop on top of St Peter's in Rome."

"The Nuns shop?" Said Jill and I in unison.

"Yeah." Said James as though it was the most natural thing in the world. "The Nuns Shop. Go up on to the roof of St Peter's and there you'll find a shop selling God's bric-a-brac. It's run by nuns. Honest!"

"I don't believe you. You're both as bad as each other," said Jill.

"Suit yourselves. Anyway, whose turn next to tell a ghost story? Elizabeth, tell us that one about Cowdray house you told me when we were up in Midhurst. That's a good one."

"I will, James, and you can tell the story of the ghost in the White Room at the Coaching Inn at Midhurst where we first stayed together."

"Ah!" Said Jill giving me a gentle and friendly nudge "So that's where you first got shacked up."

Oh dear. I was caught out again. If I ever return to my time I will gather up what little reputation I have and seal it in a box in the hope there will be a little left for my old age.

And so we recounted our tales. How we laughed. But as we conversed the room seemed to grow darker and each drew closer to the other; though obviously not in a way so that anyone would notice.

--~--

J.

I like ghost stories but there is a time and place for them and this old place with its flickering shadows from the oil lamps was not one of them. I was very conscious that not only were we a long way from anywhere but I didn't even know where we were. After a while Elizabeth decided that the effects of the calvados and the mirth and merriment required a visit to the loo. This was met by some laughter and to encourage her we reminded her to look out for ghosts and any bogey men who might be lurking in the shadows. Before she went I also thought it best to give advice on what to expect of French bogs by recounting one of my experiences.

I don't know whether any of you have ever visited one of those French loos on a campsite. I can tell you they require nerves of steel and extremely strong muscles in the thighs accompanied by an excellent sense of balance and should not be attempted if one has drunk more than normally required to be mildly happy. They consist of a wooden cubicle from which you can watch the stars if it is not cloudy or raining. This box has a small hole in the floor, on either side of which are two raised plinths for your feet. The meaning of these becomes apparent later. A large cistern hangs above and if you are lucky a chain is attached to the ballcock lever, for without it one must jump in the air to reach it. After one has completed one's ablutions and if required, finished using the month old copy of Le Figaro thoughtfully provided by the campsite patron, a difficult operation is then required. Firstly, ON NO ACCOUNT must the ballcock lever be pulled until you have positively established that the door is unlocked and can be opened easily. It is also important to ascertain whether the door opens inwards or outwards otherwise severe bruising can occur. Then holding your breath, you must simultaneously pull the lever, leap from the plinth, push open the door and run as fast as you can. For up from the floor like a bubbling cauldron the cistern will discharge a huge deluge of water which firstly submerges the plinths and then follows you for some distance across the field!

--~--

E.

With James' instructions in mind and fearing my lack of training in such matters, I proceeded to the loo which thankfully I found was not only inside and had a roof but also blessed with a more modern arrangement. It had a large plate glass window which, while it allowed one to view the countryside, it conversely and rather disconcertingly also allowed any person outside to view the interior and the activity within. Unfortunately, my relief was only temporary as just as I had settled myself I heard what I thought were footsteps on the gravel outside.

--~--

J.

The first we knew of Elizabeth's plight was when the living room door burst open and Elizabeth cried "There is something or someone outside!" At first we thought this was another ghost story but when we regarded the distress on her face our laughter stopped in an instance. The silence was deafening save for the footsteps on the gravel. I could sense from the ladies that they expected some manly act to be performed such as to go and investigate the cause of the noise. Immediately in response Sean reached for his cigarettes for courage. "Damn. I've run out of fags again but luckily by good fortune I have a backup supply."

Then as if by magic Sean produced from his pocket a little pouch tied by a string and a packet of Rizzlas. He undid the pouch and poured what looked like a very, very dry tobacco into an open paper. I remember buying a bag of this awful stuff in my smoking days at college. As a student I found one could save money for beer by buying rollups. I was told that rolling a fag was a simple operation for any man who wished to impress a lady with his "fingerative" abilities, but this particular dry tobacco had to be treated with care. For those of you considering taking up this occupation I will give some advice, if not warning.

First, the tobacco must be gently poured onto the paper then carefully rolled and sealed using the tongue to wet the gum. At all costs the "cigarette" must be kept horizontal at all times. Any slight incline and the dry tobacco will fall out of the tube. This presents a number of difficulties when smoking said cigarette. Talking and gesticulating while smoking is out of the question. Also it must be rolled to an exact tightness. If too loose, you take a drag and the whole tube of tobacco is sucked into your mouth causing more exclamations than a lady would normally expect to hear from a man in her presence. Too little tobacco and when you "light up" the whole damn thing bursts into flames singeing severely your moustache which, fashion dictated, I was growing with some success at the time to impress the fairer sex. If this was not enough I found that sometimes the paper would stick to my lips. On trying to remove the abominable thing from my mouth for the simple purpose of imparting wisdom or philosophical gems to impress a girl I fancied, the result was the fingers would slide down to the end of the tube pinching off the hot ember, burning my hand and then falling into my beer!

I remember such an occurrence once while driving after an exceedingly late evening. The ember fell between my legs. Where it disappeared to I know not but it caused me intense panic and a considerable amount of erratic driving before I screeched to a halt, jumped out of the car and spent some considerable time examining the clothing of my nether regions very closely.

But I digress again. Where was I? Oh yes, I remember. Elizabeth had heard what she thought were footsteps outside and action was required. Of course all we had to do was wait until the morning but after hearing such a noise this waiting for the morrow before investigation began seemed an extraordinarily long time for the ladies. Action was required now, they said. Unfortunately, Sean whose last rollup had ignited in his face took this as a sign that the best course of action was to search the whole mill for anything that might contain nicotine. And by the light of candles and oil lamps he opened up any cupboards and boxes he could find until he found two old cigars in a box. They looked like they may have been there since the time of Mr Raleigh, but they were cigars! He was so pleased with this that when he offered me one I accepted. Aah, the pleasure of lighting up! Actually this pleasure lasted about two seconds before I felt my burning lungs collapsing under the foul smoke, resulting in a coughing fit in which I thought I was going to breathe my last.

--~--

E.

I do feel that James is heavily influenced at times by Sean and I hoped his rather prolonged coughing fit on inhaling the smoke from what I can only describe as piece of old hemp would encourage him to be more reticent in joining in Sean's capers in future.

After he had recovered, I reminded them once again of the footsteps. So staying very close together all four of us carefully explored the mill until it became apparent during our wanderings that the footsteps came not from outside but from behind the two large wooden doors which partitioned our living room from the barn! The Something or Someone was in the house!

--~--

J.

With a quick drag on our cigars which distinctly began to smell of an old dung heap accompanied by another round of coughing Sean and I decided we must go and look behind the doors. Why? Well, because in all the horror movies that's what the hero had to do. The ladies immediately grabbed us in a fashion that would have met with the approval of Jane Austen, and Elizabeth pleaded, "Please, please don't go! You don't know who might be there. We will be all alone and we may be ravished by someone not to our liking!" But we gentlemen knew our duty.

Sean slowly withdrew the rusty bolt on the barn door and armed only with an oil lamp and two evil smelling cigars I followed him into the unknown. For it is only polite that the eldest should go first. The sound grew closer and then suddenly by the dying light of the lamp we saw what it was. Two great rats were eating the grain. Our courage returned (NOT that it had gone very far away despite what might have been said later by our slanderous companions) and we retraced our steps slowly back to the mysteriously re-bolted barn door, forgetting that the ladies did not know we were returning. All they heard was the sound of footsteps getting closer and CLOSER!

After we had apologised for the tenth time and promised to buy them new under garments at the earliest opportunity, they forgave us for scaring the proverbial out of them.

--~--

E.

So having nearly burnt the place down, frightened ourselves with ghost stories, chased away the rats and opened a window to let out the foul smelling cigar smoke we decided it was time for bed. There was much discussion about which room we should sleep in and who should go first and who should stay in the cosy, warm and well-lit living room. Sean said we should toss a coin for it which unfortunately resulted in James and I being winning the bed chamber. I am still convinced Sean had secreted a double-headed coin in his trousers.

The bedroom contained one of those wooden box beds. You know the ones, they are designed to stop rats climbing into bed with you and gorging on your eyeballs while you sleep. As we got in I chanced to look up and saw a picture on the wall. It was Grandma! It was one of those pictures where the eyes follow you around the room. For some reason I felt she was giving us a disapproving look. How she knew we were not yet married I do not know. Worse, I espied a small door in the corner of the room which I could have easily believed in the darkness was a gateway to hell and prayed that it was locked and the key was lost. However, James said he did not trust in prayers and decided to test it himself to allay my fears only to find that on close inspection there was no key, no lock and it opened to the outside of the house! As you can imagine it was a restless night. Every time we awoke, there was Grandma staring at us. If this was not bad enough at one moment my wits almost left me completely when James remarked that although the bed was very cosy there was still plenty of room for Grandma to climb in beside us!

--~--

J,

Ah, morning! What a wonderful time it is. Though on this particular morning I felt the large bruise on my arm in response to my little ghostly joke was a little uncalled for.

The sunlight shining through the morning mist over the mill pond quickly dispersed the ghouls and ghosts of the night. After breakfast the mechanic arrived with the good news that our car was ready. And so with not too much regret we left Grandma's Mill.

Until this day I don't know the location of the place.

We eventually arrived back in Paris a little later than expected after Sean 'accidently' took a detour through the Bois de Boulogne to view *les femmes de la nuit*. As we settled down on in our apartment enjoying the comfort of electricity and running hot water Sean said.

"You know that was a strange old place, Jimbo. I kept on drifting in out of sleep all night."

"Us too. Got woke up by weird noises like rats in the rafters scurrying about."

"Yeah. Mind you one time when I woke up I nearly had the fright of my life when I saw Elizabeth wrapped in an old shawl and funny laced night cap quietly sneaking back into your room from the loo."

"I can assure you, Sean, wild horses would not have enticed her out of that bed in the middle of the night... Oh my God! What did you say?"

"What's the matter?" Said Jill, "You both look like you've seen a ghost!"

--~--

The End

A Holiday in Cornwall

E.

Daymer Bay lies on the estuary of the River Camel and according to a brochure we had found it is famed for its miles of beautiful sandy beaches and warm waters. It is also said to be a tranquil place where one can enjoy a pleasant vacation and lead a quiet existence.

We had rented rooms in a Manor House located in what James described as a perfect village. By which he means one consisting of nothing but an old church and an inn whose sole purpose is to supply James and Sean with copious quantities of cask conditioned ale preferably cooked by a master brewer on his own premises not twenty yards away and using water transported magically from a highland spring.

--~--

J.

The house nestling in a steep valley with its own secluded gardens was over two hundred years old and had rooms converted into an apartment which the owner rented out to guests. Just as the brochure said it combined an idyllic setting with all the comforts that modern amenities could offer. Having duly unpacked we drove into Wadebridge for provisions and as it was quite late in the day decided to eat at an Italian restaurant by the river. It was quite dark by the time we finished and had some difficulty finding the house again as the satnav, without any prompting from us, had decided to take an economical route which avoided anything that normally classified as a road. We quickly discovered it is a requirement in North Cornwall that all roads must be no more than twelve feet wide, bend in a different direction every fifty yards with no apparent reason and must be sunk so far below the surrounding fields that no view of any landscape is possible to aid direction. In case the occupants of a vehicle can read a map the tracks are also occasionally punctuated at junctions, which appear out of nowhere, by white finger posts pointing in any direction other than the ones printed on the 'fingers'. Sean believes that this was done during the last war to confuse any invasion force and had not been fixed since. I was of the opinion, having done it myself, that it was a prank by young boys to confuse tourists. This provoked much discussion if not argument on our map reading abilities not helped by the fact that on one occasion we found ourselves back in Wadebridge. We eventually returned to the house quite late after inexplicably passing its entrance twice and on entering it was unanimously agreed that it was thought best to forget about the evening and retire straight to bed where I fell straight to sleep. The absence of traffic and street lighting had a most soporific effect on me because I slept like a log until nine in the morning when the smell of frying bacon rose me from my slumbers.

--~--

E.

I awoke after a delicious sleep to sunbeams falling and dancing on the floor from a small gap in the curtain. James I noticed had already risen and by the aroma coming from the kitchen I presumed a full breakfast had beckoned him in preference to me. After breakfast and our menfolk had 'volunteered' to wash up we promenaded around the gardens and relaxed on some old seats in the apple orchard to enjoy the sunshine. My mind filled with a day of gentle strolls with James beside me by the sea. However, Sean and James had other plans. We discovered they had planned a surprise camping trip and had purchased what they described as a large two roomed tent for this purpose. Apparently they had decided that we should completely renounce the world for a couple of days and commune with nature. Jill said she could easily commune with nature by looking out of the window of the living room and I supported her by reminding them that having taken almost fifteen hundred years to reestablish a modicum of civilisation after the Romans left and learnt to build, thanks to the re-discovery of Vitruvius, reasonable warm and dry abodes, I had no idea why anyone wanted to return to the experiences of primitive man and live in the middle of a field with only a bedsheet for protection from the elements. Nevertheless, the idea of such a life style had great appeal to our menfolk and so having bought adequate provisions from the local town we drove down to a field by the sea and joined a throng of other 'happy campers'.

Why Jill and I agreed so quickly to this mad idea I am at a loss but if any ladies reading this can explain how our sex acquiesces so quickly to the suggestions of men and have a solution to prevent it I would be grateful if they could send a letter to me post haste.

--~--

J.

We managed to find a nice quiet corner of the field to pitch our tent away from yapping dogs and screaming children and also up wind from the toilet block though we continued to have some difficulty persuading the girls this was better than the manor house we had left.

--~--

E.

By reference to a small booklet Sean and James attempted to construct the tent while we ladies assumed our natural role of preparing diner. I must admit I was not well versed in the art of cookery but

Jill was very helpful in showing me how to open a tin of beans and to prick and cook eight sausages on two little gas stoves. I began to have a much greater respect for the skills of my cook at Hamgreen and also the merits of cooking in a sheltered place such as indoors where a breeze does not direct the flame to anywhere but the item needing heating. After about half an hour when we noticed that the tents' construction was progressing nearly as fast as our cooking our menfolk suggested it might be helpful to drink some bottled beer. I had noticed while buying provisions that James and Sean had procured a large white box in the grocery shop which they took it on themselves to manhandle to the car while we carried the other foods. This large box now appeared from which Sean retrieved four bottles. James handed me one. I now found myself, Elizabeth Bicester, daughter to the squire of Hamgreen, sitting in a field with an orange sheet for shelter, holding a frying pan in one hand spitting fat in all directions and drinking beer directly out of a bottle with the other. However, just as I began to wonder how I had got here and whether that manor house we had left was all a dream from another world I felt a drop of water splash on my face, then another.

--~--

J.

The sausages were well cooked and not too blackened on one side. Elizabeth apologised for her performance and hoped it would not affect any wedding prospects I had in mind, though it seemed to be said in such a way that if I ever asked her to prepare such a culinary delight again the realisation of that prospect would become vanishingly small.

We managed to scrape most of the beans out of the pot. I was a little envious of the people in the bigger tent next to us who had brought what I can only describe as a full range cooker from which drifted towards us the aroma of a full curry which became more delicious and enticing as dusk approached. This was not helped by the rain which the morning's weather forecaster and his super computer had failed to predict.

After we had eaten we drank some more beer. As our two torches were failing we decided to retire early. We agreed unanimously not to change into pyjamas, mainly because we had forgotten them, and went directly to bed where we were able to enjoy the sound of the various radios and televisions emanating from the surrounding tents.

--~--

E.

Despite being assured that the quilted bag I had squeezed into was the bedding of choice of adventurers ascending the Matterhorn, I felt its makers had not taken into account the inclement weather of an English summer's evening for the cold damp air outside aided by the rain was slowly percolating through the material into my body. I mentioned this to James who demonstrated his consideration for me by suggesting we join our bags and climb in together to

148

share our warmth. The torch had now failed and it took some contortions and fine work to climb onto one divan and join the bags. Eventually after many manoeuvres which seemed to require more intimate entwining than I thought necessary we were eventually 'zipped up' inside save for our two heads which competed for a coat and my jacket for pillows. This improved the situation sufficiently for me to be able to decline his invitation to remove all our clothing for extra warmth.

About midnight James decided to pay a visit to the toilets, no doubt due to the number of bottles of beer he had drunk. Unfortunately, we found the fastening of the bag had become caught in the material and the key to the fastener lay on the outside possibly because, as I found out later, in the dark we had managed to join the sacks inside out. To open the fastenings seemed a simple task except now we discovered our arms were trapped inside the bag. Try as we might we could not escape. After not a little struggling James, and not I, I wish to add for the record, managed to upturn the fragile divan and deposited us still inside the sack on to the ground. I thus found myself in the pitch black laying on top of James in a position I would not normally expect to find myself in, in the middle of field or anywhere else come to think of it and accompanied by the sound from another tent of what seemed to be a radio playing a rendering of 'The Ride of the Valkyries' but was actually a recording of a combo I believe called 'Lead Metal Zeppelin'.

--~--

J.

For some reason I felt a cold shiver as though someone had poured water on my back and my head felt distinctly wet. With Elizabeth on top of me I couldn't move so I turned my head slowly fearing I had badly cut myself only to push my face into ice cold water. I realised that Sean's choice of the nice sheltered hollow where we had pitched the tent was also the watershed for the surrounding hills and our sleeping bag was lying in a small channel of running water. I decided to call for help. There was no answer. I whispered as loud as a I could. Somewhere a Jack Russell decided to join in.

Eventually Jill appeared. It was still pitch black.

"What's the matter, Jim? Good God, why am I standing in water? Where are you?"

"Here." I whispered helpfully in the darkness.

"Where? Oh! What are you doing down there? Oh sorry, Elizabeth, I didn't recognise your bum. Where's Jim?"

"Underneath me. We can't move!"

"Please don't tell me you're stuck in that position. There's no way I'm going to be the one who's going to call the ambulance and explain what's happened."

"We can't get out of the sack!" I said, "Our arms are stuck inside."

"And you got poor Elizabeth to fall for the oldest campsite trick in the world. Did Jim tell you that you'd be much warmer if you climbed into his sleeping bag?"

"And how many times have you fallen for that, Jill?" I said.

"Shut up!"

"Every time I ask," sniggered Sean from the other side of the partition who obviously had been listening.

"Elizabeth, a word of advice. Never get inside a sleeping bag with a man. Now let's get you out. There, got it! Well at least you had the sense to keep your clothes on."

--~--

E.

Having extracted ourselves from the bags we decided to abandon this place and gathering up our wet clothes returned to the manor house where we could commune with a nature with which we were more familiar.

--~--

J.

The following day we thought Elizabeth's suggestion of a quiet gentle stroll along the cliffs admiring the views followed by a nice long lunch at our expense in Polzeath seemed an excellent idea. In fact, Sean and I thought that any other idea the girls came up with would be brilliant as well and agreed we would follow their instructions to the letter without complaint.

--~--

E.

After a pleasant day in which normality was restored and the recurring vision of my father discovering me in that 'position' of the previous night abated, Sean and

151

James decided to make amends and treat us to dinner at the local inn which was only about four hundred yards from our house; though I suspected their real intention was to make sure the local beer had been kept well and in cask condition. However, we did not complain as cooked food and washing up by some else seemed quite attractive.

I had succumbed to a pair of jeans which I had to admit had great practicability at times. I had bought them at an "end of season" sale at an emporium in Chichester. James who thought he would come along to 'help' admitted later that until we had entered the premises he had presumed he could not get enough of scantily dressed ladies. However, the madness that confronted us on entering the hall changed his opinion. Apparently although such places are adequately provided with private changing rooms the lure of a bargain and the fear of it being snatched away seemed to have turned the fairer sex into vicious vixens who in order to try on their items of choice were prepared to strip in the shopping aisles rather than risk another taking it from them. A pair of suitable jeans were eventually found at the expense of much bruising and I am rather afraid to say cross words on my part directed at a pair of ladies of a certain age with their skirts half tucked in the back of their underwear who thought said jeans would fit them.

But I digress again. Although the inn was not far it did involve a walk down a dark lane with the noise of a stream close by and hidden in the trees. As we approached Sean and I espied what we thought was a young girl in a grey-white hooded coat walking towards us. As we got nearer she turned and literally disappeared into the wall of the vicarage.

"Did you see that?" Said Sean.

"What?" said James who had busy making sword play with the beam of his torch with Sean's.

"The girl! She was just there then she turned and vanished."

"OK, Sean. Save it for the walk back after a few beers."

"No, I saw her too." I said, "She just disappeared into the wall."

We quickly walked over to the wall and shone our torches along it until we found an old boarded up door. James tried it but from the amount of ivy growing on it, it looked like it hadn't been opened for years.

We carried on to the inn.

--~--

J.

We entered the main bar where I was confronted with about a dozen firkins of Cornwall's finest beer which by their beckoning appearance had been prepared especially for Sean and me. We decided we would start at opposite ends and meet in the middle. After sampling the first pint of the delicious brews Elizabeth reminded me of the other purpose of coming here, that is the promise of a slap up meal at our expense and that Jill and she would be extremely grateful if we would order a table.

While still at the bar Sean asked about the girl we had seen. The bartender who was clean-shaven save for two great side whiskers no doubt styled to aid drinking the local elixir said he wasn't aware of anybody but pointed to an old chap by the fireplace who looked like his dad as being a person with more knowledge of the area.

We walked over to him and asked if he knew about the girl. He didn't seem to forthcoming until noticing his pint was nearly empty I offered to buy him another one. For some surprising reason he instantly perked up a bit.

"Thanks." Taking a good quantity of the glass in one gulp. "All I know is it could have been a ghost of the girl found here."

We all crowded round to listen. For there is nothing like being told a good ghost story in some small hamlet miles from anywhere and before a long walk home in the dark.

"Why do you think that?" Said Sean to encourage him for he thought the English always needed help in embellishing to make a good story.

"Eh. Oh. It was in the 70s and workmen were digging up the floor just where you're standing, darlin', to fit a new drain."

He pointed to where Elizabeth was who immediately let out a gasp and jumped about two feet back. Seeing his performance was going better than expected he continued.

"When they got down about three feet they found a

skeleton of girl. Cor! There was ructions, police an' all. But they got the county alchohologist to 'ave a look at 'er and he found she was about a hundred years old."

"What happened to her?"

"They buried her in the church next door. Gave her a good funeral."

"No, I mean what happened to her to be where she was?"

"Dunno. Expect it was one of them squires at the Manor knocked up a maid and got rid of her before the missus found out."

"Have you seen her?" Sean asked mischievously. The old man looked up.

"She's about sometimes," he said slowly, looking at the fire. "Everyone calls her Adele. By the by, youse the ones staying up the Manor?"

"Yes, why?"

His eyes lit up. I could see his evening was going well.

"I've heard people staying there hear strange noises at night."

Oh dear, it was time to feed the grockles some good scary stories.

"What sort of noises?" I said.

"Nothing much. Last people said it's like scratching or knocking coming from behind the walls."

"Well, we were there last night and heard nothing."

"Expect they like to let you settle in first."

He was certainly playing it well. He looked at his now empty glass and then at me.

"I could tell you more if you like?"

I was in half a mind to buy him another pint when the waiter interrupted us and said our table was ready.

--~--

E.

It was a most enjoyable evening and after wine and beer Jill and I began to regard the previous night's escapade as an almost enjoyable caper.

The only disappointment for Sean and James was that they were unable to reach the middle of the line of barrels before the bar closed for the night but they promised the publican faithfully they would return the following evening and complete their mission. Normally on a dark evening one expects to be escorted home safely by a gentleman but on this evening we decided that if we ever going to reach the house without falling in the stream it was best if Jill and I firmly held and escorted the gentlemen. To thank us on this promenade our menfolk decided to provided us with entertainment in the form of two or three ribald songs the contents of which I will not record here. Suffice to say they mainly involved the exploits of an Eskimo called Nell and her prodigious bedroom antics.

We eventually got them into to bed and despite the ghost stories we heard nothing that night.

--~--

J.

After another excellent day in which we found doing what we were told worked to great advantage Sean and I thought that we would give the girls a treat by cooking for them. We got the biggest pot we could find and made stew and dumplings accompanied by some reasonably expensive wine.

This went down well and I think we were almost forgiven for the camping incident.

As we sat back complimenting each other on what perfect couples we were and how unlucky everyone else was not knowing us a strange scratching sound came from the wall behind Elizabeth.

--~--

E.

As I sat back at the dining table feeling rather full from taking too many dumplings and enjoying what I regarded as quite a good wine by James' standards I heard behind me above the fire place a strange rustling sound. It was like someone or something scratching or scraping behind the wall. I noticed the others had sat up and were looking behind me. I turned round slowly. The wine and food had dulled my senses a little but not sufficiently to stop the fear bubbling up inside me for the noise was getting louder and nearer. Then suddenly there was a great commotion coming from the chimney. Dust, soot and blackened rubbish fell into the grate. Then a pigeon.

"My God, it's a pigeon! Oh god, a bird in the house. Help me!" shouted James and curled up in a ball in the floor.

"What's the matter, James?" I cried.

"He has a pathological fear of flying birds in a house." Said Jill.

Sean walked over to it and gave it a kick.

"Sean, don't! It must have got stuck in the chimney, poor thing."

"Well, it's dead now."

After a few moments we calmed down and James uncurled himself. But just as we thought we could relax the scraping started again. An uncontrollable shiver ran up my spine and I flung myself at James wrapping my arms tightly around him. Then more soot fell into the grate followed by the BIGGEST rat I had ever seen!

Pandemonium! All four of us were up on the table in an instant. Both Jill and I holding our skirts tightly about our knees and our menfolk, I was disappointed to find, were holding us in a way which suggested they were using us for protection. What a tableau this would have presented to any one passing the window. Round the room the rat scurried. Then it jumped on a chair, stood on its hind legs and looked straight at us before leaping between Sean's legs, creating screams which must have been heard in the inn.

--~--

J.

A bird in the house and I will die on the spot but a rat is just a large mouse. Letting go of Elizabeth I jumped down and opened the kitchen door and then the back door. The rat shot out the house like hell was following it. When I returned I was the hero of the hour.

"Oh, James, what bravery!" was the unanimous response from the girls. But just as I was contemplating what just rewards I deserved for this Sean ruined my moment. "Where's the pigeon?"

The brief sense of bravery dissipated instantly to be replaced by panic. The grate was empty! I looked around the room and to my horror found it staring at me from the curtain rail very much alive and giving me the distinct impression it held me personally responsible for having trapped it in the chimney.

Before I could shout it flew straight over me, causing me to duck and bang my head on the table, before flying off round the room while I flew out of the door.

--~--

E.

I found James under the bed clothes. I pulled back the covers to find him curled up with his eyes shut tight.

"Has it gone, Elizabeth?"

I noticed a nice bruise was forming on his forehead but felt it best not to draw attention to it. He took a little convincing but eventually he believed that the bird was out of the house thanks to Jill who had grabbed it and carried it to the back door.

I undressed and climbed into bed with him.

"You know, James, I think I have had enough holiday. Can we go home tomorrow?"

--~--

J.

The next morning when we eventually gathered our wits we decided that the pleasant and tranquil coast of Cornwall was not for us and left as quickly as we could.

If you ever come across the person who wrote the nice promotional holiday brochure for the River Camel and its surrounds, please let me know his name and address so I can denounce him under the Marketing Standards Act.

--~--

The End

In the Beginning. Or Was It?

It depends where you start

:*Addendum 7 to the Report on the Time Travel Diaries*
Originator
Professor Rolleston. Weber Institute, Mons Olympus, Mars.
Date 24:16: 2025

In my original publication of the diaries I recorded that I had found them bound together in a copper chest during an auction sale at Miss Bicester's home at Hamgreen. However, I omitted the circumstances by which I became aware of their existence.

The reason was simple. I had been charged with making sense of the diaries and assembling them into a chronological order and this task kept me fully occupied for over a year. However, as I progressed through the diaries I began to feel that they were not just a record of the time travellers' lives but something more. They seemed to have a life of their own and I began to wonder whether the means by which they came to my attention was a necessary and integral part of their existence!

I could not put my finger on it at first until I came across an entry in Miss Bicester's diary regarding a discussion where she and Mr Urquhart wondered whether they were actually real and had free will or were under the influence of unknown forces. They were concerned that during their journeys through time they were not in control of their actions. They were especially suspicious of

H G Wells who often appeared at opportune moments to nudge them in a certain direction to assist with a quest and had great interest in their diaries. I must confess he is an enigma for he states in one entry that he has the ability to have what he referred to as 'out of time' experiences and see the future! I have gleamed a little from the Martians on this and gathered that not only is he well known to them, but I have the distinct impression that they often assist him or use him to alter futures or pasts for their own benefit.

However Miss Bicester's entry fed upon my unease for it suggested that the diaries somehow dictated rather than recorded their action. In other words the time travellers were or are constrained within a time-trap from which they are unable to escape.

As I pondered on this, the unusual means by which I became involved with the diaries began to prey on my mind and I began to wonder whether I was part of the diaries as well. Because of this I believe it would be helpful if I present a brief resume of how I arrived at the diaries in the hope that it may shed further light on their importance.

--~--

--~--

In the Beginning. Or Was It?

As you are aware, before my arrival at the Institute in 2021 by means of the Time Cavern at Midhurst, I was engaged by my old University in Dublin to study the myths and legends of the ancient Irish races.

That was in the year, 1895. You may remember that was also the year that Mr Wells published his memoirs of his travels through time.

As part of my researches for the University I visited many of those burial mounds in Ireland which are recorded as being the abodes of their gods. And it was in one of those ancient tombs where I first came in contact with them.

You can imagine, even in the learned society of my age, it was one thing to study the stories of ancient races but another to admit meeting them!

It was late summer of that year and the new term was approaching and I had still not completed a small thesis on the folklore of the West Coast of Ireland in which the Dean of my College had expressed some interest. By early September I had exhausted the University's library's stock of information on the subject and decided that the best course of action was to visit Dingle to obtain first-hand knowledge of the archaeological sites which are so numerous on that wild peninsular. As time was pressing I decided to take the newly opened railway from Tralee. However it was a journey so fraught with twists and turns through mountainous passes and over precipices that I

163

promised myself, if I wished to have a long life, that I would return to Tralee by coach.

On arrival the town of Dingle did not fare better for the stench from the mackerel and herring canneries pervaded everywhere and it was with relief I escaped the following morning by means of a dog cart, hired for a pittance, into the countryside.

It was a beautiful day and having visited the famous Galarus church and the nearby *clachans* I decided to visit the remains of the old promontory fort of Dunbeg, now sadly lost to the ravages of the sea, which according to the antiquarian Du Noyer contained a souterrain. I had spent a number of hours looking for the fort without success and as it was getting late in the day I decided to call upon a croft in the vicinity in the hope of obtaining directions. An old lady came to the door wrapped in a coarse woollen shawl. She had a face wizened by a life time's exposure to the Atlantic gales and wore an expression of one who did not welcome visitors. In reply to my enquiry regarding the fort's location she crossed herself and muttered in Irish that it was not a safe place as it was occupied by the fairies. This was not the first time I had heard this on my travels in Ireland and I persisted with my request until eventually, though reluctantly, she pointed to an old grass track leading to the cliff edge.

I tethered the horse's reins to a tree by the road and took the path. After crossing two rough grass fields I eventually espied the stone wall of the fort. As I approached it I noticed near the entrance adjacent to the path a shaded patch a few feet across. On closer examination I discovered it was a depression within which was a stone walled shaft. Thinking it might be the souterrain I decided to climb down. The hole was quite small, no more than three feet square but I succeeded, after removing my knapsack, to squeeze into it. It was not deep for I landed on my feet with my head still above ground. I was about to conclude it was the remains of a well when I noticed a similar sized horizontal stone lined passage at the bottom, its roof at a level with my waist. However, just then the light faded and looking up I saw the sun which was quite low in the sky had become obscured by dark grey clouds. Fearing I might be caught in one of those deluges for which the island is famous I decided I would leave and return in the morning when I could explore it at my leisure by daylight. As I was about to clamber out I heard a rustling sound within the passage.

My immediate thought was that I had disturbed a rat or bird. Most people, I am sure would have left quickly at this point but my curiosity had the better of me and I found myself peering into the passage to see what was there. There seemed to be an orange glowing mist. Thinking it was a trick of the light I took a closer look and saw something white and vaguely rabbit-shaped coming towards me. I confess at that moment fear took the better of curiosity and I sought escape. I clambered out of the hollow and almost ran back across the fields to my dog cart which thankfully was still tethered to the post and drove post haste back to Dingle. While I jogged along in the cart, I cursed myself for my weakness, and tried to make sense of the shape I had seen, for although rabbit-shaped I felt certain it had been no breed of rabbit I had ever encountered before. As curiosity surmounted fear, I resolved to turn back and investigate further, but my resolve never grew to a sufficient dimension to actually instruct my nag to turn around.

At the hostelry the owner inquired of my day and on replying that I had visited Dunbeg, he asked if I had seen anything unusual there. I was taken aback for I did not want the locals thinking I had seen the Fairy Folk. But I am sure he noticed for when I said I had not he gave me a knowing smile and a wink. I quickly changed the subject by asking if there was any post for me as before leaving Dublin I had requested the Post Office forward my mail. He rummaged through a cardboard box and eventually found a white envelope. I examined the postmark and noticed it was from England but posted two weeks before my arrival. I did not understand how it had arrived there as I had only chosen the hostelry the week before.

I thanked him and retired to my room where I immediately opened the letter and found it was from a Squire Bicester of the Lodge at Hamgreen, Sussex. It said:

Dear Professor Rolleston,

If you come across a small White Rabbit or Cat in your travels, we would be very interested to hear from you at my home to recount your experiences.

Yours sincerely
Alfred Bicester, Esq.
The Lodge,
Hamgreen,
Sussex.

PTO.'

I turned the paper over and found a detailed map of how to get to Hamgreen from Chichester.

As you can imagine I was at a loss. For he had described what I had just seen. I had intended to make further exploration of the mysterious tunnel but now my curiosity was engaged with this new puzzle. I decided to curtail my visit in Ireland for the moment, and after sending a letter of acceptance of his offer, journeyed to England the next day.

I arrived at Chichester within a few days by a more civilised railway and took lodgings at the Fountain on South Street near the railway station. After a beef pie which had more crust than meat I walked up to the Cross to take a cab to Hamgreen. However I had difficulty finding a driver to take me as none had heard of it. Eventually after showing a young lad Mr Bicester's map and offering a ridiculous fare for the journey he agreed on the proviso that he could copy the map so he could find his way home.

The journey although uneventful followed forest roads after we left Cocking and required frequent halts to consult the map. Subsequently it was early evening when the cab dropped me at the courtyard of the house. I had sympathy with the cab man when he refused to wait for fear of getting lost in the dark.

Squire Bicester's home was one of those old Georgian piles complete with ashlar walls and crenulations. Virginia creepers, already turning Autumn red, covered much of the front façade. As I approached the main porch across the gravel a light appeared in a window. A few moments later the front door opened and an elderly gentleman appeared in evening suit, who on seeing me, smiled and said these exact words:

"Good Evening, Professor Rolleston. I am Alfred Bicester. We wondered when you would arrive."

I was dumfounded and seeing that I was not in a fit state to reply he gently took my arm and led me into the house where he introduced me to another gentleman, Mr Wells, also dressed in evening attire.

For the next three hours during which I joined them at dinner, they quizzed me on my knowledge of the Irish Gods, their abodes and the folklores and fairy tales associated with them while Mr Wells took copious notes. All my questions regarding the letter were politely deflected.

Mr Wells asked me if I would be willing to provide a comprehensive list of the chambered burial mounds I had visited along with a brief description and whether they were accessible. He was particularly interested in any folk tales regarding 'the little people'.

I was still in a state of mild shock and found myself acquiescing to his offer, though not before enquiring why they were of interest to them. In reply, Mr Wells rose from the table and beckoned to me to the drawing room where next to the fireplace against the wall stood a large oblong black mirror over four feet wide. He then picked up a small plate with many different coloured buttons and pointing at the mirror, pressed one. Immediately moving images appeared of two people! One, a lady in Victorian dress and another whom I can only describe as a hatless man in a poacher's outfit! They seemed to be in the middle of an altercation in a field where a cricket match was in progress. After a few moments the man rose from his seat and walked away across the field. The lady looked perplexed. Then the image vanished and the mirror returned to its black colour.

I turned to Mr Wells for an explanation who said the images were captured in the year 1873 and the gentleman was James Urquhart and the lady was the daughter of Mr Bicester, both of whom shortly after disappeared. I did not understand the significance of his remark and asked what the images meant. He said all would be revealed if I returned for an auction which was to be held at the house the following Saturday and to go to the attic where I would find the diaries of the two people I saw in the black mirror. When I asked why I could not see them then he replied that they had not arrived yet. But before I could ask why, Mr Bicester interjected reminding us that the evening was getting late and as the road was quite poor he advised that I stay overnight and return to Chichester in the morning. After the excitement of the day it was easy to accept his kind invitation.

The next morning I returned to Chichester by a dog cart provided by Mr Bicester and driven by an old servant.

When I arrived I immediately purchased the local broadsheet and found an announcement for the auction at the Lodge at Hamgreen on Saturday. By this time I felt that I had been cast on a ship without control of its destination nor means of escape.

On the day of the auction I arose from a rather sleepless night in which small creatures filled my imagination and after partaking of a hearty breakfast I went to the taxi rank and sought out the cabbie who had taken me to Hamgreen the night before.

Thankfully his return journey from Hamgreen had been uneventful and as a consequence he was easily persuaded. When I arrived at the lodge a dozen people were already there examining the furniture and sundries. I looked for Mr Bicester and Mr Wells but they were nowhere to be found.

I enquired of the auctioneer regarding their whereabouts, but he replied that he was under instructions from a local solicitor and had no knowledge of them. I then pretended to idly peruse the lots until I had the opportunity to enter the house via a side entrance without notice. I found myself in a green wallpapered hallway with three doors. With no idea what I would say if I met someone I opened each door in turn and was gratified to find a stair in the third. I climbed it as quietly as possible and came out on to a long panelled corridor with doors on either side which I presumed led to bedrooms. At the end I saw a small staircase. Hoping that it led to the attic and no one would appear from any of the rooms I tiptoed down the corridor as quietly as possible and quickly climbed the wooden steps only to be confronted by what I presumed was a locked door. I hastily fiddled with the latch to no avail. In desperation I gently applied my weight to the door and to my relief it opened. Inside was a small room illuminated by a fanlight and lined with dusty shelves of books and papers. My elation in finding the attic was quickly arrested when I realised I did not know what I was looking for.

I swiftly scanned the shelves fearing that at any moment someone would enter and find me for I could not think of an excuse as to why I was there. Then I noticed a copper box on a pile of papers. I undid the clasp and found two notebooks. I opened the first and to my relief found it was written by Elizabeth Bicester, the other by James Urquhart. I had found them! However I was now confronted with the problem of how to remove the box and its contents undetected from the house for I did not wish to lose them to another in the auction. Although the diaries had become of immense importance to me, I was unsure as to the importance of the chest. An idea came to me. I decide to remove the diaries from the box, put them in my coat and replace them with a couple of similar sized books from the shelves. I quickly selected a small book on architecture by Ruskin and a dog-eared volume of the Ingoldsby Legends. I then returned downstairs to the auctioneer to ask a price for the box. When he asked what was in it, I replied that it contained just a couple of books but I had taken a fancy to the box itself. He took it from me and opened it. He looked at the two books and said that under auction rules I must bid for it and the contents and added it to the auction list. Not wishing to argue I agreed.

At the auction I bid just five shillings in the hope of not bringing attention to myself but to my surprise another gentleman bid as well and offered five pounds! I declined further bidding and the gentleman took his prize and immediately opened the box. I could tell from his expression that he did not expect what he found. He turned around and saw me looking at him. I smiled and shrugged my shoulders as though my loss was of no consequence. He was not amused. Embarrassed by what I had done I wanted to leave there and then but I decided the best thing to do to allay suspicion was to bid for other items and I eventually walked away with a cheap copy of Scott's Ivanhoe and Charles Darwin's infamous book.

At the end of the auction when I rose to leave, to my

consternation, he followed and accosting me in the courtyard asked why I wished to have the box and the books! I replied that it was the design of the box that interested me and thought it would make a good cigar case for the Drawing Room. He regarded me rather intently for a moment then asked if I had looked inside the box. I replied, perhaps a little too hotly, that I regarded his question and his implication rather impertinent but gave him the names of the books that were in it. He hesitated before bidding me a curt good day and summoning one of the cabs in the courtyard. I waited until he left before I took a cab back to the Fountain.

When I arrived I almost ran to my room, locked the door, removed the two notebooks from my coat, sat down on the only chair and began to read.

Their contents were perplexing. One, a rough notebook by a James Urquhart, was a diary written in rather an undisciplined scrawl and contained entries dated in the year 2015! The other was a leather hand-tooled diary of Squire Bicester's daughter, Elizabeth Bicester. The dates of her entries were 1870-1873.

At first I presumed Urquhart was using a cypher for his dates for both the diaries seemed to recording the same events. I decided to lay them both side by side on the bed and compare page by page. To my surprise they tallied almost exactly day by day. But as I delved further I realised to my amazement that they were also describing travelling backwards and forwards in time! My immediate conclusion was that this was an elaborate hoax. Then I remembered Mr Bicester had mentioned that his daughter had disappeared and I thought perhaps she had eloped with Urquhart and knowing she had written a diary hoped it might provide some clue to her whereabouts.

I sat back digesting this and idly turning the pages wondering what Mr Bicester would make of this fantasy when to my amazement I arrived at a page in Mr Urquhart's diary which described their contact with creatures like the one I had seen at Dunbeg! I quickly turned to Miss Bicester's diary and found the same description. Furthermore, they both claimed the creatures were from the planet Mars! This was beyond belief for until then I had presumed they had collaborated on a fantasy in the manner of Mr Jules Verne.

Nevertheless, I continued reading and making notes until the faded light required a candle.

At about eight o'clock there was a knock on the door. I quickly hid the diaries in my coat, in a dread that the gentleman who had challenged me at Hamgreen had somehow tracked me down, but when I unlocked and opened the door I found to my relief it was Squire Bicester.

He was equally relieved to find I had the diaries and even more so when I gave him his daughter's to read. He turned the pages avidly and with much affection, stopping here and there with a smile. He then handed it back to me and asked me if I would like to examine them more closely and compile a book of their contents. From what I had read I was only too willing to accept his offer for I was now convinced the diaries were more than fantasy. He was gratified by my reply and in return treated me to dinner in the saloon bar. Afterwards, he invited me to meet him the following day at the church of St Denys in Midhurst at eleven o'clock where there would be an opportunity to further my researches. By now my curiosity had the better of me again and I accepted his invitation with some enthusiasm.

I arrived at the church the next day at the appointed time and found him sitting in a pew near the entrance of the nave. After greeting me and ascertaining that I had the diaries, he then took me down to the entrance of the crypt where he removed two altar candles from a box adjacent to the door. and lighting both gave one to me. By their light we crossed the crypt to a small wooden, studded door. He lifted the latch and opened it to reveal a stone-walled passage. He entered and beckoned me to follow. What opportunity he had for me in such a place I had no idea but after the strange events I had experienced I found myself following him willingly without question.

After about fifty yards we came to a blank wall. It was smooth like a white metal. He then turned to me and said that what I was about to see I must not fear. Unfortunately this was precisely the emotion his comment caused and was compounded when he walked straight through the wall and disappeared! I looked back down the passage now illuminated by my solitary candle and my shadow flickering eerily on the walls. I only hesitated for a moment before strengthening my resolve and followed where he went.

I appeared, with relief, in one piece and without injury in a small illuminated cavern littered with electrical glowing devices. Mr Bicester was nowhere to be found. But by one of the machines stood Mr Wells who, on seeing me, immediately asked me if I had the diaries.

My first concern was naturally for Mr Bicester but Mr Wells assured me that he was safe and I would meet with him again soon. He then repeated his question.

On hearing my reply he asked if I was still willing to continue my researches. I nodded and removing the diaries from my coat showed them to him as I presumed he wished to examine them but instead he turned to a desk and pulled a lever. A humming sound which I had heard on entering increased in volume a little. Suddenly part of the cavern wall turned black in the shape of a door. Mr Wells invited me to go through. Once again I hesitated but only for a moment.

I was now standing in an orange-lit room lined with dark mirrors. In front of them, sitting on a row of desks were three people in blue boiler suits manipulating levers and dials. Every now and then moving images of two people would appear briefly on the mirrors. I immediately recognised them as Mr Urquhart and Miss Bicester.

But what made me exclaim rather loudly was the small white creature which seemed to flit from mirror to mirror studying the images intently. It was difficult to focus on it for it only seemed to appear from the corner of my eyes Suddenly one of the gentleman, who must have heard me, looked in my direction. I recognised him immediately. It was the man who had tried to buy the diaries! I turned around to speak to Mr Wells but he had not followed me. I had now lost both my companions in this adventure. I tried to return through the door to the cavern but it was not there. I was trapped! A wave of panic washed over me but to my surprise the gentleman was smiling. He walked over to me and putting out his hand introduced himself as Mr Batalia, a Director of the Weber Institute. He was most apologetic for his manners at the house for he had not realised I was on the same quest. I enquired what quest he thought I was on. To which he replied the same as mine and then asked if he could see the diaries. I feigned ignorance for I still did not trust him. He looked me in the eye for a moment then seeing I was not to be persuaded, shrugged his shoulders and said it was of no consequence. All he wished was that I stay a while on Mars at my own free will and study the diaries and write a report on my findings.

Up to this point no one had mentioned Mars and at first I thought I had misheard him. When he saw my confusion he took me over to a black mirror and, after adjusting some dials, an incredible view of a blue sphere in a black sky came into view. "Our planet, Earth, as seen from Mars!" he declared.

I stood there mesmerised at this incredible scene

until he then diverted my attention to the adjacent mirror where he showed a landscape of rust-coloured, rock-covered desert from which rose three impossibly high volcanoes. Above them hung two tiny silver moons. "Mars!" he declared.

If I had just arrived out of thin air from my home to this place I would have regarded the vision as some form of trickery but after the experience of the journey I had taken, I found myself ready to believe with no further proof that I was now on the red planet.

But more was to come for Mr Batalia now informed me that I had arrived, by God knows what trickery, in the year 2021!

This was the final straw for by now my nerves had reached the end of their tether. I confronted him, rather rudely and insisted he return me to Earth and my time immediately and preferably to my home in Dublin. But instead of arguing with me to stay, he sighed and pressed a mark on the wall behind me, and the black door appeared again. Without an adieu I rushed through it and was gratified to find myself in the cavern again with Mr Wells standing there.

Once I had gathered my wits I recounted my experience and asked him to remove me from this madness and take me back into my own world. He could see I was much agitated. After a moment's hesitation he took out his fob watch and after looking at it and, after adjusting some controls on one of the illuminated desks, agreed with my request. However, as it was rather late he would recommend that we return to Hamgreen first as the last train had left Midhurst and then make arrangements for my return home the following day. Seeing no alternative practical solution and remembering that I had left my baggage there, I reluctantly agreed.

Mr Bicester was waiting for us at the lodge and after taking us into the parlour, brought us a supper of ham sandwiches.

I recounted my experience to Mr Bicester, including my visit to Mars, which did not seem to surprise him.

When I had finished they both sat silent for a minute then Mr Wells said that although he respected my request to go home he wished that I contemplate a little on what I had seen because the safety of our two planets would depend on the analysis of the diaries and in his opinion there was no better man than I to fulfil that function.

I replied that I could not see how this was true for I was just a simple professor and he would be better off with a person who had an understanding of time and interplanetary travel. However it seemed that the fact that I had seen the Martian at Dunbeg gave me a considerable advantage over others, though he did not explain how.

He also suggested that I might find answers to my research on the folk tales of the country. But when I described Mr Batalia's interest in the diaries he frowned and drawing me closer whispered that I should be wary of Mr Batalia and keep the diaries close.

I was not to be persuaded and insisted on leaving for home the next day. To their merit they did not press me further and the following morning I bid them adieu and took the trains to Fishguard and hence to Dublin.

Almost a week passed before the white creatures ceased to haunt my dreams and I felt a sufficient semblance of normality to allow me to return to the university to complete my thesis. I had only two weeks left to complete it and I immediately began but to my consternation found that all I could think about were the diaries and after two days I had written nothing more than one side of foolscap! I went out for a walk to clear my head but to no avail for I am sure I espied once or twice a small white creature in a cloister window. By the time I returned I knew that somehow I was entrapped within their web.

An opportunity had arrived which might not visit me twice. I sat down and wrote a letter to Mr Bicester.

I will not recount the return journey I took nor how I arrived on Mars again in 2021, but for the following year there I analysed the contents of the diaries and by means of the cavern and help from Mr Wells, I journeyed back and forth between Mars and Earth gathering information on the burial mounds of the British Isles.

Mr Batalia took great interest and constantly requested reports on my progress. Sometimes with much excitement he would bring me fragments of the diaries he claimed he had found and asked me to resolve their meaning. But I was careful what I gave him, for I had discovered that he appeared in the diaries in an unfavourable light. It seemed that he was attempting to stop Mr Urquhart and Miss Bicester from travelling in time. At one point he brought a paper from a Mr Maxwell. He was quite agitated and wished to know if it contained a key to travelling through time. Unfortunately, or perhaps fortuitously, it contained mathematical formulae which was beyond my comprehension and he left disappointed.

One evening, while reading in my room, I noticed out of the corner of my eye a movement by the table and turning saw one of the white creatures sitting there. It did not seem to have solid substance but as though it was having difficulty staying in the present for it flickered. It had two small wings which shimmered. For a moment I felt myself in a trance and when I woke up the creature had disappeared. A few minutes later Mr Batalia entered my room without knocking and asked if I had had a conversation with a Martian. I described what had just happened. He told me that my researches had come to the attention of the Martian delegation at the Weber Institute and they were going to provide me with what they called a space-time portal to try to contact the time-travelling diary writers.

It took a while to locate the couple for they were constantly moving back and forth in time but I eventually found them in a certain time line, and with the Martians and help from Mr Wells we set up controls which allowed the transmission and recording of their diaries, as has been documented elsewhere. The system is rather unstable and unfortunately the recordings of their travels often appear randomly from different timelines which necessitates considerable work in identifying their correct origins and the order in which they are written.

Nevertheless, although I have accumulated a considerable number of diary entries, the reason for the couple's ability to travel in time and across time still remains an enigma. It has been established that it originated at the time of the reconstruction of the Martian portals between Mars and Earth. It is thought that the activation of the portals created small eddies or vortices in the space time continuum which percolate unpredictably around our two worlds and in which Mr Urquhart and Miss Bicester became inexorably entwined.

There are, however, certain locations in these webs of time which contain stability. They are difficult to describe but I have been told by Mr Batalia that they may be analogous to the Lagrangian nodes that exist around two planets where the gravitational, or in this case, the time fields are neutralised. In particular, I discovered that Elizabeth Bicester's house at Hamgreen seems to be the central node in the distortions which in some time lines has portals to the past and future. It may form a nexus between Mars and Earth for on occasions parts of it will be found temporarily on Mars.

There is a strange phenomenon attached to it. The inside of the house is often in a time stasis caught in the year 1895 but part of the building also inexplicably existing far into the past and future. Why this year in particular I do not know though I have read that Mr Wells helped an injured Martian who fell from the sky in that year and shortly after he published his time machine book.

Another important node apparently exists beneath the old castle at Midhurst which the travellers refer to as the Time Cavern. It holds a machine that can with the right skills move in both time and space. Mr Batalia claims he was involved in its construction but I believe his machine only works because it taps in to the time node that exists there already.

But my real concern is with the Martians. What are they doing and what do they want from us? I have read in the diaries that they invaded Earth. In another they were thwarted before they could begin. Which is true? Perhaps both. I have gleamed that they move through time like us but exist a little in the future and the past simultaneously. Perhaps they can also move across time. Mr Wells believes that they can see many futures and somehow can choose which one to take. But it is impossible to know for certain for we cannot communicate with them. Only through their trance-induced dreams can we glean a little of what they think.

I know they have taken great interest in the diaries and, in particular, the time travellers, whom I believe they are using to influence the future. But what future and does it include the human race? I am sure Earth is still attractive to them for Mars, despite the restoration of the ancient Martian seas and atmosphere, is small and the ice caps are returning.

The diaries are the key but like Elizabeth I wonder whether they actually record their time travels or dictate what they do. Are we just puppets compelled to follow the book with no free will? Perhaps we will never know.

I am reminded of those lines in FitzGerald's translation of the Rubyat of Omar Khyam.

There was a Door to which I found no Key.
There was a Veil through which I could not see.
Some little Talk awhile of Me and Thee
And then no more of Thee and Me.

The End

Moon Shadows

*Moon Shadows first appeared in A Feast of Christmas
Stories: Unwrap a Sussex Tale.*

The night before Christmas is not the best time of the year
for your car to break down, with no phone signal, on a
lonely country lane in deepest Sussex.

After my fourth attempt to start the engine the electrics
died completely. Black. Pitch black. Not even a glow from
the dashboard. After a while, my eyes became accustomed
to the darkness, and through the windscreen I could just
make out the sunken road, its banks lined with overhanging
trees.

I needed a light. I searched through the car, and with
relief, found my old bicycle lamp in the glove box and
switched it on. The breath from my exertions in the cooling
air had formed an opaque mist on the windows, which in
the torch light seemed to enclose the car around me like a
tomb. I quickly wiped the windscreen with my hand to see
out, and to my horror, saw a distorted face staring back at
me!

It took a second to realise it was my own illuminated
reflection, and a little longer for my heart to stop racing.

I looked at the dead dashboard again and, swearing
heavily, I tried once more to start the engine. Nothing. So,
I decided to get out and find some help.

An ice-cold wind hit me which blew swirls of dead leaves into the car. I shut the door and swung the lamp around to get my bearings, but could see nothing except the tarmac road and the white fingers of naked beech roots climbing up the banks. As I moved away from the car I noticed a strange light bathe the road, and looking up, saw through the swaying black tendrils of the trees, a full moon racing across the sky between fleece-white, ragged clouds.

Which way? I had not seen a house for miles since crossing the old stone bridge at Stedham. Reasoning that there had to be one soon, I grabbed my coat from the car and took the direction I had been driving. As I walked along the road, glistening patches of frost appeared and disappeared between the moon shadows cast by the trees. After about a hundred yards, the shifting black shapes caused by the torchlight unnerved me, and I turned off the lamp and let the moon guide me.

It was then I saw the white signpost.

A woman was standing next to it in a hooded cloak. Its colour, if it had any, was washed away by the moon. Trying not to frighten her, I shouted. "Hello!" But she didn't hear me in the wind. I approached closer and tried again. "Excuse me, but my car's broken down."

She turned. Her face was pale in the moonlight, but her eyes were soft and strangely welcoming.

"Oh, that often happens here," she said with a smile.

"I see. Is there a house round here where I could get help?"

"Perhaps at Iping but they'll all be abed, for the moon is up and they'll want to be asleep when he arrives. Mine is nearer if you wish."

And without another word she turned onto a footpath I

hadn't seen and disappeared.

Seeing nothing else to do, I followed.

It was more of a deer track than a footpath. I chased after her with my torch, trying to avoid the overhead branches and tripping on hidden roots. When I eventually caught up with her, I said, "Do you live close to here?"

"Of sorts." she replied, "But when the moon is here it is easier to stay."

"What do you mean?"

'It is the light that helps. What do you need?"

"I want to phone a garage."

"Oh, you shouldn't worry about that. I am sure it will all be better in the morning."

But before I could ask what she meant I heard the tinkling of bells, far off beyond the woods. She turned in its direction and said, "We must make haste if we are to get home before the moon sets. You can see it is in a hurry tonight."

I looked up. It did indeed seem to be in a hurry.

As I followed her along the path I heard, almost muffled by the wind, the faint sound of bells again. It seemed to be coming from above the trees and had a strangely familiar jangling rhythm, but when I looked up I saw nothing but the moon darting between the swaying branches.

The frosted air was seeping through my coat and I began to wonder why I'd let myself follow her down the path instead of going to Iping. Then, just when I had almost made up my mind to turn back and take my chances on the road, I saw a light through the trees.

"Is that your house?" I said.

"It might be. Let me see."

She looked up at the moon. "Yes, that seems to be about

right."

The cottage was old, with flint walls and Sussex tiling. By the porch, lit by twinkling fairy lamps, a window glowed with the light of a flickering fire. In the cold it seemed homely and welcoming. She went up to the door, opened it, then turning to me, said, "Quickly, come in, he is nearly here!"

I found myself in a single living room with white plaster walls and in the centre an old wooden table with two large plates. On the stove by the window, was a large skillet from which came the delicious aroma of roasting meat and chestnuts.

She removed her cloak, revealing a long red and gold dress embroidered with dancing hares entwined with wildflowers and green vines.

"That is beautiful." I said.

"Thank you." She smiled with pleasure and her eyes met mine. Soft familiar eyes that drew me to her. In the light of the fire her face momentarily reminded me of someone or something from a time past. But before I could think what it was she went over to the stove, bent over the skillet and said, "Ah, dinner is ready. Now sit down and I'll pour you some wine."

"Who's the other plate for?" I said.

"For you."

"You knew I was coming?"

"Not always. It depends on the light."

She placed the roasted meat on a board and brought it to the table.

"There, perfect and just in time. Do you want to carve? You always like to."

"OK, so what's going on?" I said, "You appear out of

nowhere and then bring me here as though it was the most natural thing in the world."

"I didn't bring you. You came of your own accord. And to answer your question: have you forgotten I am your wife?"

"What?"

"Oh dear. You don't remember, do you? You are always surprised to see me. Well, what must be said must be said again."

Coming up close to me she tentatively placed her hand on my shoulder. "We were in the car driving home."

Her hand tightened on my shoulder. "You had a heart attack. You died a year ago."

I looked up in disbelief. "Died! What do you mean?"

"I tried to save you - but I couldn't, and I ran down the road for help. Then when I got to the signpost, I saw you in the moonlight coming towards me. I was so frightened. Oh, the relief to see you! But you didn't recognise me. I thought you had amnesia from the accident, so I brought you home and put you to bed, but in the morning when I woke, you were gone."

"What are you talking about?"

"That's all I remember. Each full moon I find myself waiting for you at the signpost and if the light is right you come to me. Not always. Sometimes you recognise me. Other times, well, like now. It took a while before I realised that I had died in the car as well."

"This is ridiculous. I don't know what you're playing at. You're mad - I'm going!"

As I tried to leave, she grabbed my arm. "You have said that many times. But you always return."

I pulled her hand roughly away, ignoring the pleading look

189

in her eyes, and ran out of the house without looking back, and down the path.

The full moon was now low in the sky and it was getting darker. A hanging blackthorn branch tore at my coat and, as I tried to remove it, a sudden thought came to me. If the moon was setting, then it was nearly dawn. Impossible! I'd only left the car about half an hour ago. I checked my watch. A quarter to midnight. So the moon should have been overhead! What was going on? But my only thought now was to escape this madness and find the local village she said was nearby.

Eventually, I found the road and ran to the signpost expecting to find the direction to Iping. But its three white fingers were blank! I decided to go back to my car in the hope the engine would start again.

To my relief it was still there, parked in a layby and covered in white frost. But as I approached it I noticed there was something wrong. Very wrong. One tyre was flat and the windscreen was smashed. The silver-blue paint was flaking with rust and covered in dead leaves and debris. I checked the number plate. It was definitely my car. I tried the door. It was jammed. I yanked it again and it opened, revealing in the torchlight an old bird's nest on the seat. I shut the door quickly. My back shivered with a cold, clammy sweat.

Then her words hit me like a bolt. "You died a year ago."

And as if to reinforce those awful words a bough creaked and cracked in the wind above me and fell with a crunch on the car.

I ran like the wind back down the road.

The moon had nearly set, and I could hear that tinkling sound again. It was getting louder and closer behind me. I looked back and nearly jumped out my skin as a group of heavily antlered deer leapt silently out of the trees, closely followed by what seemed to be an open carriage and vanished into the darkness. I shook my head in disbelief. I wanted nothing more than to be out of these woods and somewhere safe and warm. If the demons of Hell had been behind me I could not have run faster. At the signpost, I dived into the undergrowth looking for the footpath. I hacked at the branches, stumbling on roots in panic. Moon shadows leapt towards me like dead hands trying to draw me from the path. Finally, to my relief, I saw the light of the cottage again.

She was standing at the open porch door, lit by the fairy lamps which cast coloured patterns on her dress. It may have been the cold playing tricks on my eyes but, just for a moment, their flickering glow seemed to bring the embroidered hares to life. Before I could catch my breath to speak, she said, "I knew you would come back." And she wrapped her arms around me. For only a second I hesitated, then I returned her embrace and a familiar fragrance washed over me. I knew who she was.

"Now come in, my love." she whispered, "Don't be scared. We have the whole night together again."

I entered in a daze and removed my coat to feel the warmth of the fire. Then I slowly walked over to the table, my heart still racing from my flight and sat down.

She brought her chair round and sat next to me. Her hand grasped mine and I felt an immense calm. The wind ceased to play on the windows and a strange silence and stillness pervaded the room. Even the flickering shadows cast by the fire seemed to fade away into nothingness. I sat mesmerised as my memory of her slowly returned and I immersed myself in its joy.

A noise outside broke my reverie. The sound of many hooves and tinkling bells, then silence...then footsteps, slow, measured footsteps, approaching on the gravel path. The footsteps stopped. Silence. Then three knocks on the door accompanied by a jolly laugh, as familiar as childhood.

I turned towards the door then back to her "Please don't tell me..." I stuttered in disbelief "Is that who I think it is?"

"Yes." She whispered. "I wished for you and he brought you to me. My Christmas present. Now fetch that warm mead and mince pie by the fire. I think he deserves a treat. Don't you?"

The End

Other books by the Author

from the
Time Travel Diaries of James Urquhart and Elizabeth
Bicester

Book 1 Out of Time

The first diaries of the humorous and sometimes romantic
time travel adventures of James Urquhart, science lecturer
living in 2015 and Elizabeth Bicester, Victorian Cambridge
graduate, whom he met at a cricket match at Hamgreen in
1873.
Despite their banter regarding each other's manners they
manage through incredible feats of illogical deduction and
with not a little help from James Maxwell, H. G. Wells, the
Martians and some strange time devices, to save the world.

Book 2 A Drift Out of Time

In this volume, they have returned home to find they are
not only in an alternative future but a different aspect of
themselves. To get back to their world they must travel
between Mars and Earth, drifting across time and space,
until eventually they reach home and discover what the
Martians really are.

Book 3 A House Out of Time

Once again, the intrepid couple have "retired" to a quiet
life of ease in an alternative world after helping the Martians
save the Earth and their own planet. Unfortunately,
Elizabeth thought it would be a good idea to visit her
ancestral home at Hamgreen to see what had become of it.
Such is the curiosity of women…

Book 4 The Space Between Time

In these extracts from the Time Travel Diaries we find the intrepid couple enjoying a peaceful and romantic picnic by the River Rother when a motor launch turns up captained by Mr Wells.

Apparently, a certain Mr Tesla has conducted one of his electro-magnetic experiments which has fractured time and dumped everyone in an alternative world from 1895. The problem is that only a few people have noticed the difference.

Mr Wells wondered if James and Elizabeth would like to help.

Book 5 The Time Place of Mars

If you are taking your Victorian wife to a car wash for the first time, it's a good idea to explain beforehand that the long blue furry cloths banging on the windows are not aliens trying to abduct her.

This will give you more time to think of a reason why both of you are suddenly transported to a palace on Mars where Time stands still, and you're surrounded by twelve strangely magical statues of mythological Gods.

Luckily Mr Puddlewick, a bank teller from Threadneedle Street is on hand to help. Even though he has no idea, after attending a lecture by Mr Tesla in New York on communicating with Mars, why he is there.

All he knows, apart from what is behind the frescos on the walls of the Palace, is that he found a strange device which had a picture of Elizabeth and I with a message "Get Urquhart".

So, he pressed the Red Button.

About the Author

Bruce is a retired health physicist who lives on the south coast of England, just a few minutes' walk from the sea. When he's not researching King Arthur, he's out walking on the South Downs with his wife and friends trying to remember all the names of the flowers and mushrooms his wife has identified.

When it's raining he can be found sometimes in his "upstairs shed" as his wife calls his study, trying to master new jazz chords.

A life of writing scientific reports and reading early science fiction, especially the genre of time travel such as the works of Anderson, Simak and Wells encouraged him to start writing his own novels about the adventures of a modern man and a Victorian lady who meet at a cricket match in 1873.

His stories have been described as "Tom Holt meets P.G. Wodehouse meets Philip K. Dick meets Fortean Times."

You can get more information on this and his other books and hobbies at his blog at:

www.timetraveldiaries.co.uk

Or you can visit our website at:

www.aldwickpublishing.com